6

Priscilla qu
inside, reas ... **d**
strength.

They rode the elevator to the second floor, then walked to the nursery window.

"There they are," Pete said. "One, two, three and four."

"Oh," she said, "they're cherubs."

No one could resist such sweet and tiny babies. Their tiny fannies wore small diapers. Impossibly small arms each had a hospital-issued bracelet identifying them. Adorable caps of different colors adorned their heads. They each wore a small T-shirt and had a blanket, though one of the girls had kicked her blanket off.

All of them slept peacefully, unaware of the two adults staring at them through the nursery window.

Pete was a tempting man—tempting enough to marry. And who wouldn't want to help four helpless children?

Dear Reader,

February is one of my favorite months of the year—the month of sweethearts and romantic love! It's cold outside in many parts of the world—certainly in my neck of the woods—which makes it a wonderful month for reading.

In Union Junction, it's not just the weather outside that's cold. In *The Secret Agent's Surprises*, life on the home front is going to be a little chilly until Pete Morgan makes amends with his father and develops mature relationships with his three brothers. He must also deal with his attraction to Priscilla Perkins, a manners coach and tea-shop owner. Pete's got a lot to learn if he wants to make any headway with a woman who, as he notes, is prim and proper! Used to life as a secret operative, Pete now must learn to balance family relationships, romance and—the big shocker for him—adoptive fatherhood. Pete's father, Josiah, believes Pete is just the man to go from living dangerously to changing diapers, and he encourages Pete to adopt four orphaned infants. Pete has seen his brothers Gabe and Dane fall into their father's matchmaking traps in *Texas Lullaby* and *The Texas Ranger's Twins*, so Pete knows full well he's now in a dangerous dilemma where the result may be a wedding ring and a ready-made family.

I hope you're enjoying THE MORGAN MEN miniseries. As February brings us our chilliest weather yet, I hope you'll settle in with the Morgans and their struggles to become the men their father always knew they could be.

Best wishes and much love,

Tina Leonard

Tina Leonard

POP R

Leonard, Tina
The secret agent's surprises.
2009.

Discarded by
Santa Maria Library

Orcutt Br.   SEP 2 8 2008

BRANCH COPY

GAYLORD

If you purchased this book without a cover you should be aware that this book is stolen property. It was reported as "unsold and destroyed" to the publisher, and neither the author nor the publisher has received any payment for this "stripped book."

Recycling programs
for this product may
not exist in your area.

ISBN-13: 978-0-373-75250-8
ISBN-10:   0-373-75250-4

THE SECRET AGENT'S SURPRISES

Copyright © 2009 by Tina Leonard.

All rights reserved. Except for use in any review, the reproduction or utilization of this work in whole or in part in any form by any electronic, mechanical or other means, now known or hereafter invented, including xerography, photocopying and recording, or in any information storage or retrieval system, is forbidden without the written permission of the publisher, Harlequin Enterprises Limited, 225 Duncan Mill Road, Don Mills, Ontario M3B 3K9, Canada.

This is a work of fiction. Names, characters, places and incidents are either the product of the author's imagination or are used fictitiously, and any resemblance to actual persons, living or dead, business establishments, events or locales is entirely coincidental.

This edition published by arrangement with Harlequin Books S.A.

® and TM are trademarks of the publisher. Trademarks indicated with ® are registered in the United States Patent and Trademark Office, the Canadian Trade Marks Office and in other countries.

www.eHarlequin.com

Printed in U.S.A.

ABOUT THE AUTHOR

Tina Leonard is the bestselling author of over forty projects, including a popular thirteen-book miniseries for Harlequin American Romance. Her books have made the Waldenbooks, Ingram's and Nielsen Book-scan bestseller lists. Tina feels she has been blessed with a fertile imagination and quick typing skills, excellent editors and a family who loves her career. Born on a military base, she lived in many states before eventually marrying the boy who did her crayon printing for her in the first grade. Tina believes happy endings are a wonderful part of a good life. You can visit her at www.tinaleonard.com.

Books by Tina Leonard

HARLEQUIN AMERICAN ROMANCE

†Cowboys by the Dozen
*The Tulips Saloon
**The Morgan Men

Many thanks to my editor, Kathleen Scheibling, for
steering me straight, and to Lisa, Dean
and Tim, who understand that time with family
is my personal dream

Chapter One

He who loves his son chastises him often—
Sirach 30:1, quoted often by Josiah Morgan
when his four boys rebelled against his discipline

Pete Morgan sat in a bar in Riga, Latvia, tired, cold, and annoyed as he thought about the letter he'd received from his father, Josiah, in January. The missive was a parting shot, designed to make him feel guilty. Wasn't the pen supposedly mightier than the sword?

Josiah's words hadn't had the desired effect— they had simply reignited old feelings of resentment. Pete wouldn't admit to a saint that he'd been steaming since the two letters had been found in a kitchen drawer at the Morgan ranch, one addressed to him and one to his oldest brother, Jack. Pete had left the letter for Jack with a rodeo manager, knowing it would reach him eventually.

Now it was February, and the very memory of his

father's words still set Pete's teeth on edge. He knew every word by heart.

> Dear Pete,
> Of all my sons, you were the most difficult. I saw in you an unfulfilled version of myself, a man who would never be able to settle. I write this letter knowing that you will never live at the Morgan ranch attempting to be part of the family. Like Jack, you hold long grudges. If by the time I pass on, you have not lived at the ranch for the full year, your million dollars will be split among the brothers who have fulfilled their family obligation.
> Pop

It was a kick in the teeth, not because of the money but because his father lacked trust in him, basic faith that Pete cared about his own family. Wasn't it Pop's own fault no one cared to be at the ranch or have any contact with him? It had been many years since he and his father had spoken more than ten words to each other. To receive the letter out of the blue in January had sent Pete packing to the other side of the world, even though he'd been seriously considering retirement from espionage. The life was tough, the hours and the constant danger not conducive to trust, or building friendships, or anything remotely resembling comfort. Pete used to love his job, used to enjoy the unpredictability, until recently. His last assignment had chilled him, made him search his soul.

He'd always thought of himself as a savior, rescuing people from war-torn situations. It was important, critical even, to be able to go into foreign countries and extract those who needed help. This was his way of helping keep his country safe, and he got a lot of satisfaction out of it.

The best part was knowing he'd returned a father, a mother, children, to families desperate to be reunited.

Pete had an excellent record of success, but his last mission had been beyond his control. He tried not think about it, but the shadows lurked, ever ready to assail him. He had been meant to recover fifteen children from the basement of an abandoned orphanage. But he hadn't been able to save them. There'd been bombing after bombing; the screams still cursed his sleep. He'd done what he could, but then…

Much as he might change the channel on a television set, he turned his mind from the memory of the parents who would never see their children again, shutting out the ghosts. He was haunted by his own family, and tonight he wondered if it was time to face his demons. Life was short, and it could be dark and lonely. His lips thinning, he thought about Josiah.

Jack's letter—which he'd read—had been worse:

Jack, I tried to be a good father. I tried to save you from yourself. In the end, I realized you are

too different from me. But I've always been
proud of my firstborn son.
Pop

That was Pop, always playing the Morgan
brothers off one another, which was how the trouble
had begun so many years ago, driving a wedge
between Jack and himself that still existed today.

His other two brothers, Gabriel and Dane, had
made up with the old man. They'd married, had
children. Collected their million dollars.

But now the stakes were higher. Pop no longer
resided in France in the knight's templary he'd purchased. Pop had come home to live at the Morgan
ranch to enjoy the new additions to his family, especially his grandchildren, which he'd netted with all
his matchmaking and millions.

If Pop thought Pete had any intention of living
under the same roof with him, he was mistaken. Pete
would rather sit burning in the darkest corner of hell
before that happened.

No woman, no family, no million dollars, would
ever tie him to the ornery son of a gun who was his
father. Pop had foretold the future ominously—
Pete would never settle down. He did indeed hold
long grudges—he'd learned it from the master. His
father, Josiah.

There was nothing more satisfying than being the
blackest sheep in the family.

PRISCILLA PERKINS looked at the older gentleman who'd seated himself in her tea-shop-and-etiquette studio in Fort Wylie, Texas. Long of limb, strong as an ox though showing some signs of aging, Josiah Morgan was a commanding presence. He wore a black felt cowboy hat. His hair streamed long and gray to his shoulders. The jeans and shirt he wore were clean and nice enough for a meal in the city.

"I'm glad to finally meet you in person," Priscilla said. "I've heard a lot of good things about you, Mr. Morgan." She noticed that Mr. Morgan didn't seem to feel at all out of place in the dainty surroundings. He took the tiny, floral-decorated china cup she handed him and drank the tea, his sharp gaze considering her.

"You were at my son Dane's wedding," Mr. Morgan said, "and I asked his bride, Suzy, who you were. I like to know everyone who is a friend of the family."

Josiah hadn't met many of the people at Suzy Winterstone's and Dane Morgan's wedding. They hadn't expected him to return from France for the wedding. He'd ridden in at the last second, a flamboyant mirage on the horizon, to witness his son's nuptials. His sudden appearance had given everyone in Union Junction quite a shock, not the least of all his son Pete.

Pete Morgan had disappeared before his brother's wedding, and Suzy had told Priscilla they'd probably never see Pete again. *Which will teach me,* Priscilla thought, *to keep myself crush-free in the future when it comes to handsome, devil-may-care types.* "I'm sure you're not here for etiquette lessons, Mr. Morgan, and I suspect you have no need of my party-planning services nor any of my specialty teas and cookies. So what can I do for you?"

His grin sent a tingle down her back. It was amazing how much Pete resembled his father—maybe it was his confidence, maybe it was the rascal shining through. Priscilla suspected it would be a good idea to stay on her guard.

"You may have heard that I'm a meddler," Josiah said with a wink.

"No," Priscilla said firmly. "What I've heard is that you are very generous to the town of Union Junction, and that you don't necessarily get along with your four sons."

He gave a bark of laughter, amused by her boldness. "True enough, all of it. They say the more money you give away, the more comes back to you. Certainly that's held true for me. Of course, I also suspect that you're fibbing just a little in the interest of good manners, girl. Even *I've* heard that I'm a selfish ol' pain in the patoot. The town grapevine doesn't discriminate in who hears what, you know." He glanced around the room, then back at her. "You're just too well mannered to hurt an old man's feelings."

She shifted uncomfortably. Her business had definitely been growing from love and not abundant financial backing. "You're keeping me in suspense. My guess is that you haven't come here to talk about money."

"My sons, actually," he said. "Or at least one of the four."

"I'm not good with schemes that involve other people."

"And yet I understand you were staying at the ranch with Suzy Winterstone and Cricket Jasper last month. Somehow during that time, my son Dane found himself in love."

"No one can explain the human heart," Priscilla said.

He smiled. "Sometimes a man needs a little help in falling for the woman of his dreams."

"I don't know what I contributed to the situation," Priscilla said. "Otherwise I'd be running a matchmaking service instead of what I do."

"So Dane fell in love with Suzy with no help at all from you ladies."

"No help except the million dollars you promised him and your little shove in the right direction." She looked at him innocently.

He grinned. "You're not going to help me, are you."

"Not if you're asking me to somehow finagle any of your sons into something they don't want to do."

Setting his cup down, he nodded. "You know, Miss Perkins, men don't always know what they want."

She didn't say anything because she sensed a note of regret in his voice.

After a moment he sighed. "Can I tell you something in confidence?"

"Certainly."

"I'm not a well man and—" he began, but she interrupted him immediately.

"Mr. Morgan—"

"Please, call me Josiah."

"Josiah, then," she said. "I will not be a party to whatever you're cooking up. As you said, you're something of a meddler, and I do not meddle."

"It worked out for Gabriel and Laura. And Dane and Suzy. They're all happy as clams, with kids and houses and living the fairy-tale dream." His eyes twinkled and a smile played on his lips. Josiah looked pleased about his sons' new family situations.

"What exactly do you want from me? Specifically, please." Priscilla had to admit to some admiration for the man's tenacity.

"I want all my boys to be happy," Josiah said. "And happiness is finding the right woman. I had the right woman once upon a time." He stared off for a moment, then returned his gaze to her. "She's living in France now, and I'm satisfied with that. Not every man is made for marriage, and my bride was always more concerned with money than anything else, I'm honest enough to say. But I'd like my sons to have better."

"Shouldn't they figure that out on their own?"

"Maybe, but what father wants his child to

stumble?" Josiah asked, his face wreathed with quizzical thoughtfulness.

"According to gossip I've heard, you let your boys stumble plenty," Priscilla responded. "People say your boys practically raised themselves and you liked it that way."

"Sometimes a man regrets his actions," Josiah said.

"Sometimes a man never stops trying to earn forgiveness," Priscilla told him gently. "You know, you really are a nice man in your own way, but I have a life here. I have commitments, things I love. I don't have any business doing whatever it is you want from me. And you really have no right to ask anything of me, you know."

"Drat," he said. "I'd heard you might have had a tiny hankering for Pete. Scuttlebutt must have had it wrong."

"Now, Mr. Morgan—"

"Josiah," he repeated.

"Josiah, it isn't good to listen to idle gossip. You of all people should know that."

He smiled again, searching her face with keen eyes, showing no remorse at all for putting her on the spot. The wily old rancher was everything people said he was, and yet, she somehow found him endearing.

"Well," he said after a moment, "it was worth a try."

"What was worth a try?"

He stood and put out a hand so that he could gently take her hand in his. "I was hoping it was you, but there are other women who might be interested in my renegade son, Pete. He's a good-looking man—strong, tall, tough. Ladies like that sort, don't they? The strong, silent type? And yet sophisticated and endearing, like Cary Grant. Yes, I'd say the best of John Wayne and Cary Grant." He grinned at her. "I'm just the proud pop, though. Maybe women aren't looking for good-looking, strong, independent rascals anymore."

She really didn't know what to say to such audacity. There was no doubt Pete was a sexy man. She'd been wildly attracted to him when she'd met him in January. He was indeed very handsome, and his devil-may-care attitude drew her in. Tall, long-haired, with eyes of glacial blue—his very face spelled danger. She shivered, remembering. He'd come across like a tough guy, but when he wanted to be charming—and he'd definitely been charming—a woman knew she'd take off her dress pretty fast for him. He'd not made any moves on her, not really. In fact, he'd seemed bent on making Dane jealous over Suzy, and so Priscilla had felt safe.

But it was the gleam in Pete's eye when he looked at her sometimes that let her know his charms could be dangerous—if he hadn't been treating her like a sister, for Suzy's sake. In other words, he was a wolf in sheep's clothing.

There was no way this would work. Josiah couldn't possibly understand. Families had their share of matchmaking enthusiasts, busybodies and downright meddlesome fussbudgets bent on having their own way. At least Josiah didn't hide his intentions. Wouldn't his scheming make Pete mad? Priscilla studied Josiah and wondered.

Was the old man really looking for forgiveness—or was Josiah angling for more grandchildren?

Chapter Two

Two days later Priscilla wasn't feeling very forgiving. Under new rules—and a revised estimation of the value of her real estate, thanks to new bank software—Priscilla learned the value of her home and business had sunk by forty thousand dollars. In the blink of an eye, she'd lost the foothold she thought she'd been gaining. Real estate was supposed to keep its value, if not go up, but with current economic conditions, banks were tightening lending standards and the way they evaluated properties.

Her situation wouldn't have been so devastating except that she'd been counting on her home to provide equity for her tea shop. The loss of forty thousand would put her out of business.

"Fine," she told her friend Deacon Cricket Jasper, who'd come over for tea and a visit. "I'll go back to doing what I was doing before I became a small businesswoman. I'll work for the government crunching numbers in some dreary office. At least I'll have some retirement funds put away."

"I don't know," Cricket said, looking around the wing of the home that served as the shop. "You've done pretty well, and this place is popular. Get an outside appraisal and ask for a home equity line of credit at a different bank."

Priscilla considered that. "No one's lending money these days, certainly not to take a chance on a tiny tea shop and etiquette lessons." The thought depressed her. Her heart was in her business. "I'd be in trouble if people were to suddenly cut back on parties and etiquette lessons for their children. Maybe it's better this way."

Cricket nodded. "One of my favorite sayings is that when God closes a door, he opens a window."

Priscilla smiled. "You're a good friend to remind me." She glanced around her pretty little shop. The walls were painted a light, cheery pink. White tables sat here and there, inviting conversation; two pink-and-white-striped antique sofas lined the walls for intimate groupings. A sparkling chandelier hung from the ceiling, illuminated by tiny purple bulbs hidden around the ceiling tray so that soft amethyst light bathed the crystals of the chandelier and reflected the hue on the ceiling. It was a comforting place. At night, when the shop was closed, she liked to sit in here with a good book, a side-table lamp lighting the pages. "It was just such a shock when I talked to the man at the bank. He was so sympathetic, but I felt bad. I'm not the only person this has happened to, so I don't intend to feel sorry for myself, but it wasn't welcome news." Priscilla took a deep breath. "However, I also liked my friends in the government office. I'll be fine."

Cricket stood and hugged her. "It will all work out. In the meantime you can always go see what Mr. Morgan had up his sleeve. There's usually money involved when he wants to pawn off one of his sons."

Priscilla laughed, surprised, and shook her head. "As much as I liked him, I fear Josiah is a one-man con game. Truthfully, the games he's up to are beyond my scope."

"Yet he has such amazing success, especially with those hardheaded boys of his. Wouldn't it be an old movie plot if he was behind this loan problem?" Cricket went out on the porch, opening her polka-dot umbrella. "This is the coldest and dreariest February I think I've ever seen in Fort Wylie."

"Mr. Morgan might be a busybody, but he wouldn't deliberately sabotage my business," Priscilla said, laughing.

"I know. I was being dramatic. I think it's the weather." Water puddled at the base of the porch as the rain came down harder.

"Drive carefully," Priscilla said. "The roads can be slick."

"I'll call you tomorrow. In the meantime, I'll be

praying for you." Cricket cast a glance back through the door longingly. "It's so comfortable in your shop that I hate to leave. I can't stand the thought that it might not be here much longer."

Priscilla waved goodbye, not sure what to say about that. She'd heard of several people in Fort Wylie having money woes—her situation was better than most.

She went inside to examine some financial statements and see what she could come up with.

PETE MORGAN sat on a military plane mulling over his prospects. The last thing he wanted was to return home to the Morgan ranch, but he'd been offered a million dollars to do so, as had his brothers. Gabe and Dane had fallen under the spell of money and lovely women, but Pete was harder, more stubborn. He wouldn't have been a secret agent if he weren't tough as steel, a trait he'd inherited from the old man. Maybe that was the only good thing he'd ever gotten from Pop. The old goat had wanted his boys tough, and that was how they'd turned out.

The oldest son, Jack, wasn't in touch with anyone in the family. He called the rodeo circuit home. Pete had no home at the moment. After he'd finished his assignment and been debriefed, he'd had time to ponder his life. He was glad he was retiring, not sorry it was all over. He was happy enough, if any of the Morgans knew what happiness was. Gabe and Dane were certainly new men since their marriages.

Maybe that was what he was missing.

Pete pushed the thought from his mind. That was Pop talking, getting in his head with his desire for more grandchildren, somehow wanting the past to be overlooked.

Pete had no intention of caving. He decided he'd find Jack, pay him a visit. Maybe he'd become a rancher like his brothers, throw in a little real-estate venturing like Pop. Surely Jack had to be getting tired, too. Pete felt his own thirty years sitting on him like a weight, or perhaps it was the traveling that had worn him down. When he was younger, his job had made him feel very important. Now he just felt exhausted. Maybe it was the absence of light in his life—and why that miserable thought made him think of Miss Manners, the wonderfully elusive and prissy Priscilla Perkins, he wasn't sure.

"WONDERED IF YOU'D ever get around to visiting me," Josiah Morgan said to Priscilla two days later, his eyes gleaming. "You're wanting to hear my plan, I expect."

"Mr. Morgan, I might just be paying a call on you to be kind. I could have a business proposition for you myself." She seated herself in the massive den of the Morgan house, located just outside Union Junction. It was different here now that Josiah had taken up residence—the house felt more like a home.

Last month, he'd been living in France. He said he'd sold his knight's templary for a handsome profit and moved back home to spend time with his new grandchildren. But while he'd been in France, Priscilla, Cricket and Suzy had spent lovely days vacationing in this house, helping Suzy keep distance between herself and Dane.

Instead of keeping their distance, Suzy and Dane had gotten married, and the women's friendships had grown stronger. Priscilla hadn't known Suzy and Cricket as well then as she did now, and the time spent together was a memory she treasured. They'd baked cookies, played with Suzy's kids, teased the Morgan brothers. "We never did get the new curtains done for this house," Priscilla said. "We meant to. We were on the way to the fabric store when we saw Jack—"

She stopped, remembering the bad blood between Josiah and his oldest son. Josiah's gaze sharpened.

"You saw my son?"

"Well, it wasn't an intentional meeting," she said hurriedly. "Now, back to your plan—"

"How did you see him? Where was he?" Josiah demanded.

"He was hitchhiking. We only saw him for a moment, truly. However, I didn't come all the way out to Union Junction to discuss Jack," she said, injecting impatience into her tone to try to move him off the personal topic she knew was painful. "Shall we get back to the purpose of your earlier visit to me?"

"How did he look?" Josiah asked, ignoring her pointed request.

"Handsome," she said simply. "Ornery. Full of life. Not interested in talking to us once he found out we were living here. He wasn't in the car long enough for us to learn much."

Josiah sighed. "So much like me."

"Handsome? Or ornery?"

He winked at her. "You're a bit of a minx, aren't you?"

"Flattery won't hurt if it gets you away from worrying about your sons. And I may as well hear your proposal. I admit to some curiosity."

"Which killed the cat, but in this case, there happen to be extra lives." Chuckling, he waved a hand to indicate that she pour the brandy sitting on a crystal tray between them. "Miss Perkins, there are four children in the county who are going into foster care. Their parents died last week in an auto accident. Very sad." He looked distressed.

"I'm sorry to hear that." She met his gaze. "Did you know them?"

"I only met the parents once when Ralph Wright came out to buy a steer from me. They lived on a neighboring ranch, you know, more homesteaders than ranchers. Young couple, big dreams. Wanted a country life for their children. They'd been trying for a child for years, it seemed. Ralph mentioned that his wife Nancy, had surgery that helped. He beamed just talking about her pregnancy. They were very much looking forward to their new family, as you might imagine." He swallowed thickly.

"That is very sad," Priscilla said, her heart breaking for the children who had lost their parents. "It's going to be very hard on the poor babies."

Josiah's expression turned crafty. "Where there's a will, there's a way, Miss Perkins. I would be interested in helping you adopt the babies."

"Me!" Priscilla's mouth dropped open. "What would I do with four children, Mr. Morgan?"

"Give them the home they need. As sad as their lives are now, I think it would be sadder to be split up in different homes, and so on and so forth." He shook his head. "Life is going to be hard enough for them."

"I don't see," Priscilla said, trying to breathe through her shock, "how you ever came to think that I would be a suitable person to adopt four children."

"As I said before," Josiah said, "I'd heard by way of a little birdie that you might have a soft spot for my son, Pete."

She blinked. "Oh, I see. You're going to do to Pete what you did to Gabe and Dane. Tie them to women with children to increase your family name." She stared at him. "Don't you think you're presuming a lot? First, that Pete would want to marry me, second, that he'd want four kids and, third, that the child-welfare agency would consider me suitable parenting material?"

"You *and* Pete," Josiah said. "Whether or not Pete would want to marry you wouldn't be the issue. Second, four kids will be a shock to his system, but talking care of that many babies would be no harder than being a secret agent. You did know that's what he does for a living, didn't you?" He watched her carefully.

"No," Priscilla said, "and I'm not sure that child-welfare services will find that comforting, either. But go on. I'm riveted by how you not only move your sons like pawns, but anyone else you decide you need."

"You're amazed that I would play God to this extent," Josiah said equitably, "and I don't blame you. But when a man has nothing left to lose, he may as well shoot for the stars. At least I do." He took a healthy swig of the amber liquid she'd poured in his glass. "Have some. It helps sometimes."

"I need clear, focused wits around you, thank you," she shot back. "You've stunned me."

"It's simple enough," Josiah said. "Pete needs to get married. I doubt you would be able to sleep knowing that four little newborns are going to be without parents when you could do something about it."

"Newborns?" Priscilla straightened. "How young are the children?"

"Sadly, only a month old."

"They're quadruplets?"

Josiah beamed. "I did mention Nancy's surgery, didn't I? Worked like a charm."

"Are they still in the hospital?"

He nodded. "That's how I learned about them. I was visiting the hospital, and the nurses were talking about the accident. So, so sad."

"Not to be rude, but do you just troll the hospital nursery looking for children and unwed mothers?" Priscilla asked.

"No," he said, laughing, not offended at all. "It's just that this time, I thought of you."

"You know nothing about me at all. I could be a horrible person."

"It's not hard to find things out in small towns." Josiah raised a glass to her. "Your parents raised you well, educated you, loved you a lot. You're very close to them, which would mean extra grandparents for these little ones. You'll need a lot of help, you know."

Astonishment held Priscilla nearly numb. "Did you have my tea shop and home business reevaluated?"

He looked at her. "What do you mean?"

"I got a notice that my home is worth less now."

"That's happening a lot in this economy. Banks don't have as much money to lend, so they're weaseling a bit." He shook his head. "No, I would never have anything to do with devaluing a property. I've made my money in commercial and private real estate around the world. I'd be the last one who would ever want to see property values depreciate." He looked at her. "Is that the real reason you came to see me?"

"I knew you were a meddler," Priscilla said, lifting

her chin, "and I suppose the thought came to mind. I apologize if it was incorrect."

"Young lady, you're entitled to think anything you want of me, but it hurts that you'd jump to such a negative conclusion." He sniffed. "Contrary to what my sons think of me, nowadays most people think I'm a pretty nice old fellow."

She held his gaze. "Josiah, you've been called a jackass by many people, pardon the term. I'm sorry if I had my doubts, but the bad news came right after your visit. I simply wondered how badly you wanted to pull your son's strings."

"You're a shrewd one, I'll give you that." He eyed her sternly. "The folks who call me a jackass are jealous, and I don't let that bother me. Some folks needed to get to know me better, and some I've had to ask for forgiveness. I can be shortsighted. But one thing I'm not is a chiseler. Anybody who's done anything I've asked has benefited enormously in the financial sense and, I'd like to think, in the emotional sense." He shifted in his armchair. "I'm hoping people will remember me fondly when I'm gone."

"I don't think you're going anywhere anytime soon," Priscilla said.

"Don't be so certain, missy. This deal I'm trying to work with you has a definite expiration date."

She sighed. "You know this is an impossible situation. Even if I wanted to be a mother to four babies, I'm not confident I could manage it. I have no experience. I wouldn't know a pacifier from a—" She stopped speaking as the front door opened. Josiah turned, his brow wrinkling.

Pete Morgan walked through the door and dropped a black duffel bag on the floor. He closed the door behind him, looking down the hallway to where he could see his father and Priscilla sitting in the den. His face was grim, an expression Priscilla hadn't seen last month. Tall and dark and beautiful, the man who'd been so playful with her and Cricket and Suzy last month was gone. In his place was a lean, well-muscled warrior with a wary expression that hinted at something dark in his soul. Priscilla shivered. She didn't think she'd feel as comfortable around him now as she had when he'd been teasing and carefree.

"Pop," Pete said. "Hello, Priscilla."

"Well, the prodigal returns," Josiah said.

Pete shook his head. "You're the prodigal. I heard you were in residence."

"I've moved back for good," Josiah said.

"Good for you," Pete said. "I won't plan on staying long, then."

Priscilla shifted, feeling awkward. "Maybe I should go."

"Maybe you should stay," Pete said. "The old man needs companionship."

"I have plenty, thank you. Gabe and Dane and their wives and children visit frequently." Josiah's expression turned cantankerous. "I suppose you only came home for your million."

Pete hesitated, glanced at Priscilla. "Darn right."

"Well. You'll have to live here with me to get it."

"That's a persuasive argument." Pete looked at Priscilla. "What would you do for a million dollars?"

Chapter Three

Priscilla stood. "I'm going to let you two go over old times. I've overstayed my welcome, anyway."

Pete looked at his father. "Don't you love the way she talks? So ladylike and proper."

Josiah grinned. "She's not hard to listen to at all."

Priscilla shook her head. "You two are cut from the same cloth. I hope you enjoy your visit together."

"Walk her to the door, Pete, will you?" Josiah shifted. "I'd get up, Miss Priscilla, but I've been tired lately."

"There he goes with his poor-pitiful-me routine," Pete said. "I hope you haven't fallen for his game."

She hesitated, glancing at his father, which made Pete wonder what they'd been discussing before his arrival. Suddenly suspicious, he whipped around to glare at Josiah. "You weren't, by chance, discussing anything to do with me, were you?"

Josiah laughed. "Ah, my son knows me too well."

"That's not funny," Pete said, feeling a slight sense

of panic. "I know what happens when you get wrapped up in our lives. Two of my brothers are married with children." He looked at Priscilla. "You don't have any children, do you?"

She blinked. He admired her long blond hair, pretty blue eyes and angelic expression—before reminding himself that the faces of angels had been known to bring good men down. He'd seen it happen often in his line of work. "You *don't* have children, do you, Miss Perkins?" he repeated more sternly.

"No," she said, her tone cool. "You know I don't."

"Well, then, stay and have dinner with us. It's sure to be an awkward affair." Pete gave her his most affable grin. "And you didn't answer my question, which I guess means you wish to take the high road and stay out of our affairs."

"What question was that?" she demanded. "You two are full of hooks and angles and thorny emotional issues."

"About whether you'd live with the old man for a year for a million dollars if you were me."

She shook her head. "You're right. I don't wish to be drawn in to your squabble. Josiah, I don't like the way you play kingmaker. Pete, I don't think you're being very courteous to your father. Bygones are sometimes best left as bygones."

Josiah sat up in his chair. "You mean, you don't think Pete should have a million dollars?"

"I don't care whether he does or not. I'm a tea connoisseur, not a family therapist."

"Well," Josiah said. "I thought she was the right woman for you, but she's not, Pete."

Pete turned to face his father, then looked back at Priscilla. "Was he trying to get you to entice me into marriage? I know it's not a polite question, but he did it to both my brothers."

"Yes." Priscilla lifted her chin to meet his gaze. "He has every intention of interfering in your life."

"And what did you tell him?" Pete asked quietly, feeling his entire body tense.

"I told him I didn't think you'd marry me, and that I didn't think you wanted to be a father to four newborns."

Pete blinked, recoiling for an instant before looking at his father. "You're crazy, you know that?"

Josiah watched the two of them carefully, his eyes hooded with interest. Then he grinned, delighted to be, Pete thought, playing the role of munificent fairy godfather. "Just hate to see four little babies without parents," Pop said, his voice all innocence. "At least you four boys had each other growing up. These Wright children will be split up." He shrugged. "I can't save the world, I know that. It was just a thought, nothing to get a brave spy like yourself in a lather over." Picking up the daily newspaper, he shook it out with exaggerated importance. "Just four little babies, counting on someone to save them," he muttered.

"I'll be going now," Priscilla said. "Welcome home, Pete. Mr. Morgan—"

"Josiah," he reminded her.

"Yes," she said. "Josiah, it was interesting to see you again."

"Again?" Pete looked at her. "When did he see you before?"

"He visited me at my tea shop."

Pete studied her before looking at his father. "You went all the way to Fort Wylie to hatch this plan?"

Josiah shrugged. "Couldn't very well do it by phone, could I? Would have been rude." He chuckled.

Pete told himself the front door was open. He could leave his father and his shenanigans behind just as easily as stand here. But he had to admit he was hooked by the game. He had a funny feeling Josiah hadn't shown all of his cards—yet. "So what did you think of my father's well-intentioned angling?"

"I think it's presumptuous."

Josiah cleared his throat, looking at Priscilla meaningfully. After a second Priscilla's face colored slightly.

"What?" Pete demanded. "Let me in on the private secret you two are sharing."

"There's nothing," Priscilla said airily, not wanting Josiah to blurt his information about her "little crush" on Pete. "Goodbye, and good luck with your mission, Josiah. Pete, good to see you again. I'll show myself out. I remember where the front door is." She hurried down the foyer hall, but Pete wasn't letting her go that easily.

"Excuse me, Pop. You and I aren't finished discussing your plot, but right now, I want to talk to her." He hurried after Priscilla, catching her in the yard. "Let me apologize for my father," he said.

"Why? He's his own man."

Pete nodded. "And everyone else's. Did he offer you money?"

"No!" Priscilla frowned at him.

"Then he was only getting warmed up. He *will* offer you money."

"It doesn't matter, Pete," she said firmly. "I'm not interested in getting married, I don't want to live in Union Junction, and you're not a man I'd consider. So it doesn't bother me how many webs he spins. I know I'm safe."

"Yeah," Pete said. "It's only my neck in the noose."

"That's true," Priscilla agreed. "I'd be willing to bet you'll be married in a month to some poor, un-suspecting girl who has no idea what she'll be getting herself into."

"Hey!" He tried not to laugh at Priscilla's forthright teasing. "Any woman would be lucky to have me."

"You forget, I've shared a roof with you. You're fun, but you're not exactly husband material."

Pete took that barb with a pang. "I know. I wish I was. But it's just not me. So, about these babies, these prize lures he's thrown out to you—"

"Don't ask me about them. You'll have to get that story from your father. All he mentioned was that he met Ralph Wright and his wife when they came to buy a steer or something. There was a car accident after the quadruplets were born. That's all I know."

He frowned. "Having quadruplets born in Union Junction would be quite an event."

"Yes. But I live in Fort Wylie, so I never heard about it. I'm sure your father is itching to tell you everything," she reminded him. She turned toward her car to open the door. "Josiah is a cute old thing in his over-eager way."

"He's a pain in the butt."

"How long are you off?" Priscilla asked.

"Off?"

"Off duty? Or whatever your break is called."

"I've served my country for many years. It's time to chart a new course in life. And there are things here I need to do." Pete caught himself staring at Priscilla's long legs, toyed with some anger with his father, felt sadness for the four babies who had no parents and realized he felt a jumble of conflicting emotions. "Maybe I shouldn't have retired so soon," he said. "I didn't factor in that with two boys down and Jack nowhere to be seen, I'll now be the sole focus of Pop's chicanery. I was hoping for some peace and quiet, to collect my million, to not think much about the old man. Now he's got me thinking about him, and you, and the kids, and his latest scheme."

"Don't think about *me*," Priscilla said, sliding into the car. "You have no idea how unavailable I am."

He leaned on her window. "Good. Keep reminding me of that."

"You bet your boots I will." Priscilla started the engine. "Take care of your father, okay? He's not as bad as you boys paint him."

"Sure he is," Pete said. "He's just got you buffaloed. He does it to everyone."

She shook her head with a smile, not believing him, and drove away.

But it was true. "I'm going to kill him," he muttered to himself, and went inside to have it out with the one person who had the power to drive him completely nuts.

His father sat in his chair dozing, or pretending to. "Pop," Pete said, "I haven't had a real conversation with you in what, ten years?"

"Your choice, not mine."

Pete took a deep breath, willing himself to be calm. "You've got to quit this obsession with family. You'll have to be satisfied that Dane and Gabe succumbed to your feudal approach to matchmaking. You're going to have to mind your own business where I'm concerned. It'll be hard for you to quit being so manipulative, but all you're going to do is make me mad as hell."

"I wasn't thinking about you, actually," Josiah said, opening his eyes. "I was thinking about the welfare of those children. I never even considered matching you and Priscilla until I heard those babies were going into foster care. They have no family, and no one around here is prepared to take on the care of four preemie newborns."

"Nor am I." Pete couldn't imagine what his father had been thinking. "I hope you noticed Priscilla wasn't exactly on board with your plan. In fact, she acted like a woman who was being offered a bad deal."

"Yeah, she didn't seem to like you as much as I'd heard she did." Josiah reached for his brandy.

His father's words caught Pete's attention. "What do you mean, you heard Priscilla liked me?" He wondered why his heart rate sped up; his whole body seemed to go on alert.

Josiah shrugged. "I heard she had a hankering for you. Usually my sources are pretty good, but this time, they clearly weren't. As far as I could tell, the lady's not interested in you one bit."

That wasn't what he wanted to hear. He was, in fact, surprisingly disappointed. "I don't know," Pete said, "we had some good times last month. There might have been something there."

"Well, it's gone now," Josiah said. "A single woman who doesn't jump at a man, a ring and four children isn't in the presence of her Prince Charming."

"You might have overplayed your hand," Pete suggested. "Maybe she's not the kind of woman who wants children."

"Every woman wants children."

"Four is a lot to start off a marriage with, don't you think?" Pete thought he couldn't handle that many; taking care of one child would probably blow his mind. "Pop, these are little people with special needs. They need to go to a family who are prepared to deal with that."

"Do you know how likely it is they'll be sent to one home?" Josiah asked. "They'll likely be separated. I hate that." He sighed deeply. "It doesn't matter. As you said, Priscilla doesn't seem to like you, so this is all moot."

"I never said Priscilla doesn't like me," Pete said. "She doesn't even know me."

"She was here with you for several days last month. Clearly that was enough for her. No, I'll have to look elsewhere to figure out how to help those babies."

"Jack?" Pete snorted. "Pop, you are never going to see Jack in this house. In fact, you'll be lucky if you ever see him anywhere."

Josiah's brow furrowed. "Every father wants to see his children before he dies, so don't dash my hopes. Someone in this county surely wants four wonderful babies, although I never said Jack was the answer."

"Well, you're not dying, so I'm not dashing anything. I'm merely stating what you know to be true about Jack."

Josiah gave him a long, considering look. "The truth is, I am dying."

Pete's insides turned to stone. "You'll have to be dragged off this earth kicking and screaming, Pop. You're going to harass us forever. Anyway, you'd never let go with two of us unwed."

Josiah shook his head. "I'm afraid I'll have to settle for a fifty percent success rate in this one thing, because the old clock of life is winding down on me."

Pete slowly realized his father was totally serious. The silence in the den felt heavy and somber; Pete could feel his heart pounding in his chest as he recognized that his father wasn't trying to manipulate him. He swallowed. "What's wrong, Pop?"

"I've had a spot of trouble with some kidney issues." Josiah shrugged. "You're the first person I've told. I think Suzy guessed, but she knew I'd talk about it in my own good time."

The anger that Pete had held close to him for so many years, the very burst of vengeful words he'd come home to loose, receded behind an emotional compartment marked To Deal with Later. "Have you seen a doctor?"

"Loads of them. There's nothing really to be done, short of a kidney transplant, and I would never ask anyone to give up a kidney for an old geezer like me. Plus, I opted to forgo the usual treatments. Basically, I came home to die."

Pete stared at his father, still looking for any sign of manipulation. For once, Josiah's face was serene and forthright. "Why are you telling me this?"

Josiah shrugged. "The times I share with my sons and their families are the times that keep me hanging on. Otherwise, I might as well be a hopeless old wrench in life's party."

"So what's the prognosis for your situation?" Pete asked, dreading the answer.

"Same outcome we'll all get eventually. Only mine will come sooner than later. Maybe a year, probably less." Josiah shifted and raised the glass of brandy. "I self-medicate. I'm not supposed to, of course. Have real medicine I'm supposed to take." He smacked his lips after he sipped his drink. "*This* is tasty medicine."

"I'll join you for a dose, then." Pete needed a stiff drink. He needed more than a drink. Pop had managed to underpin Pete's most deeply held emotions. After traveling thousands of dangerous miles and living for years nursing deep, black-edged anger, brandy wasn't going to help him much. He'd have preferred to come home and spit in the old man's eye. Now, not only did he not want to confront his father, he felt an overwhelming urge to know the real Josiah Morgan, the man whose guard was finally down and whose true heart was finally bared for all to see.

Chapter Four

"So then he wanted me to adopt four newborns," Priscilla told Cricket as they scrubbed out teapots and closed the shop for the day. It had been two days since she'd heard from Pete or Josiah—and yet she still needed time to think about what had happened. So much of what had been said was playing on her mind, drawing her thoughts over and over again to the children.

And Pete.

"Four!" Cricket exclaimed. "How can that be possible?"

"Quadruplets are rare, but not unheard of. There was a car accident and the parents were killed. It's heartbreaking." Priscilla poured fresh water over the pots and set them to dry in the rack. "I can't take on four infants, of course, but there has to be something I can do to help."

"What was Pete's reaction?"

Priscilla shook her head. "I left in a hurry. I have

no idea what was said after I was gone. With the ill will between them, I'm sure Pete wasn't thrilled to come home to discover his father was trying to serve up a wife and full family to him on a silver platter."

"Josiah is a determined man."

"He is. I'm sure he has his reasons for what he does, but I can't be a participant in his plans."

"Is Pete as hot as he was last month?" Cricket asked with a sneaky glance her friend's way.

Priscilla began wiping down tables. It had been a full day in the shop with plenty of customers who sat and lingered. She loved it when her tea room was busy. It meant a lot that her customers—many of whom were regulars and becoming her dear friends—loved her place as much as she did. Too bad the bank saw it differently. "'Hot' is an understatement," she said. "He's so hot I don't dare touch him."

"Really?" Cricket followed Priscilla, drying the tables with a soft, white towel. "Would you, under different circumstances?"

"No. There is such a thing as too much man. I, for one, am looking for a more down-to-earth, hearth-and-home type."

"That doesn't sound like any fun," Cricket teased.

"Not fun. Safe." Priscilla glanced around the room, holding her plan to her for one more moment before sharing. "I'm going to go visit the babies in the hospital."

Cricket nodded. "I figured you would. I'd like to see them, too."

"Would you?"

"Sure. Who can resist quadruplets?" Cricket shrugged. "Maybe my mommy timer is going off."

"You've never mentioned before that you had one. I thought your work as a pastor kept you too busy," Priscilla said with a smile, but Cricket shook her head.

"No one is too busy for a baby. My problem is finding Mr. Right. So for now, I wouldn't mind seeing someone else's angels." Cricket began removing the wilted roses from the bud vases, replacing them with fresh ones. "I keep wondering if there's something our church can do for them. Their care has to be outrageously expensive."

"True. Maybe we could hold a bake sale or something to raise funds." Priscilla finished wiping tables and picked up a broom. "That was another thing that surprised me about Josiah's suggestion. How in the world would I take care of four babies, when I know nothing *about* babies, much less preemies?"

"I think Mr. Morgan's intent was for you and Pete to split the duties and learn together." Cricket smiled. "I'm sure he sees himself in a benevolent role, helping people to do good work."

Priscilla thought caring for infants was probably best done by people who had some experience. "So when should we go take a peek at them?"

"Soon," Cricket said. "My baby meter says we should do it soon."

Priscilla laughed. "You could always sign up for Josiah's wedding game."

"With Pete? Nope." Cricket shook her head. "I'm afraid my eyes are elsewhere."

"You've never mentioned you had a sweetie." Priscilla stopped sweeping to stare at her friend. "Tell me!"

"It's not a sweetie, more of an unrequited longing. And I can't reveal who it is," Cricket said, "because you'd laugh."

"I wouldn't!"

"You would," Cricket assured her. "Even I know it's so crazy it could only happen by divine intervention. In the meantime I plan on sewing some little onesies for some tiny friends of ours."

The bell over the door chimed, and both women looked up. "Oh," Priscilla said, "is it that time already?"

"What time?" Cricket asked, then straightened as a tall cowboy walked in.

The man looked guarded and suspicious, a trapped animal. He glanced at the two women, then seeing the shop was empty, seemed to relax slightly.

"Hello, Jack Morgan," Priscilla said. Cricket said nothing at all.

He leaned against a wall, put his hands in his pockets. "I've met you two before."

"We picked you up a month ago when we were out shopping in Union Junction," Priscilla said.

He nodded, his gaze sliding over Cricket. "You were at the Lonely Hearts Station rodeo, too."

Cricket nodded. "Yes. I was."

The tension in the air was like snapping power lines, Priscilla thought; if this man was Deacon Cricket's secret crush, her friend must have taken leave of her steady senses.

The door swung open again, the bell tinkling to announce Pete's arrival. "Hey, everybody. It's starting to rain again, and it's colder than a witch's broom out there. I thought February in Texas would be a little warmer."

His words lightened the tension in the room slightly. "Hello, Pete," Priscilla said, wondering how a man in jeans, a basic black jacket and boots could be so mouthwateringly handsome. Line up a hundred men dressed just like that, and only Pete would make her knees weak.

He nodded at her. Her heart sank when she realized she wanted so much more than a general acknowledgment from him. This was not a man to nurse a hidden crush for.

"Hi, Cricket. Has my brother Jack introduced himself to you yet?"

"We were getting around to it," Cricket said, her eyes huge as she looked at the cowboy.

The niceties completed, the two men stared at each other for a long time. There was no hug, no handshake, Priscilla noted, just a steady eyeing.

"Nice choice for neutral territory," Jack said.

"Thanks for agreeing to meet me here," Pete replied.

"I'll just get some tea for you gentlemen, and some cookies," Priscilla said, and Cricket quickly followed her.

"Why didn't you tell me he was coming?" Cricket demanded in a rushed whisper.

"You've never cared who my customers were before," she said, gently teasing her friend. "That handsome man wearing old boots and worn-out jeans isn't anybody you'd be interested in." She put two delicate white cups on the counter for Cricket to fill. "I have no mugs to serve men with," Priscilla lamented, and then realized her friend had gone to the mirrored wall in the back of the store and was busily putting on lipstick. "What are you doing?"

"Nothing," Cricket said.

Priscilla blinked. "You've never primped for customers before."

"There's a first time for everything."

"I see," Priscilla said, and went back to the cups to fill them herself. Glancing up, she caught Cricket patting her hair. She shook her head. "I vote we declare a moratorium on Morgan men."

"I agree." Cricket glanced out the pass-through window. "They've at least sat down at a table now, instead of circling each other like wrestlers."

"That's a happy thought." Priscilla put some

cookies on a plate. "Maybe we should just stay in here and not break the flow."

"I'll serve them," Cricket said, taking the plate and swiftly leaving the room.

Priscilla smiled and put the cups and pitcher on another tray. A sweet-natured deacon and a restless cowboy—it was never going to happen.

IT WAS NEVER going to happen, Pete realized as he watched his brother walk away from Priscilla's tea shop, then climb into a brand-new black truck and speed away. Jack had heard "Pop's sick" and he'd taken off faster than wildfire. Pete couldn't blame his brother, but he'd so wanted to handle the situation better than he apparently had.

"Where'd your brother go?" Cricket asked as she approached the table.

"Back to wherever circuit-rodeo cowboys go when they're…" He was about to say *pissed*, then elected to soften his words. "When they're not interested in the topic of the day."

She set the tray down. "Oh."

The deacon sounded so disappointed that Pete glanced up. "Why?"

"I barely got to meet him, unlike the rest of your family." Cricket smiled at him. "Priscilla, you can come out of hiding."

Pete's brow furrowed. "Hiding?"

"I was trying to give you and your brother some

privacy," Priscilla said, coming in and setting another tray on the table. She sat across from him, as did Cricket. "But we can eat his cookies."

"Guess we'll have to," Pete said, taking one.

"Things didn't go well?" Priscilla asked, and he shook his head.

"Not a bit. But thanks for letting us meet here."

"No problem. Wish it had helped."

"He wouldn't have come to the ranch, and he avoids me when I try to meet him at a rodeo." Pete shrugged. "We're hardheaded in my family."

"No kidding." Priscilla poured everyone some tea and put the tray on a nearby table so they'd have elbow room. "So I've been thinking about the babies. I'm going to go by and see them."

"Oddly enough," Pete said, "I, too, have been thinking about them. I've already been by for a visit."

"You have?" Priscilla said.

Cricket asked, "Are they darling?"

"They're small," Pete said. "Tiny. I've seen, I don't know, chickens that were bigger."

"Oh, boy," Priscilla said. "Is your father still talking about them?"

"Nonstop. And you, I might add."

Priscilla blinked. "Outside of a bake sale or donating some clothes, I can't be party to any plans your father may cook up."

"Yeah, I know. I told him that. And he said he understood. Then he wanted me to tell you that he respects that a woman like you isn't interested in money."

Cricket stared at her friend. "You never said anything about money. What money?"

Priscilla shook her head. "I have no idea. We never discussed money."

Pete frowned. "Money's always first on the table with Pop when he wants something."

"Not this time," Priscilla said. "He was only offering you, I guess."

"Hey," Pete said, "don't make it sound like you drew the short straw."

Cricket helped herself to a cookie. "I have to head back to the church. It was good to see you, Pete. I'm so sorry things didn't work out better for you."

"Me, too." He got up as Cricket stood. The two women hugged goodbye, then Cricket left. Priscilla turned the shop sign to Closed and suddenly Pete found himself alone for the first time with the woman his father had proposed to on his behalf.

"Let's make a deal," Pete said.

Chapter Five

"I don't do deals," Priscilla said, "and you're starting to sound like your father."

Pete sat back down at the table. "I wouldn't ordinarily accept that as a compliment, but today I will."

Priscilla eyed him warily. Now Pete understood why his father so enjoyed the game. It was kind of interesting seeing what went on in the other person's head. Where Priscilla was concerned, he found himself *very* interested.

He supposed it had something to do with that forbidden-fruit idea women were always pushing. She'd turned down the notion of the two of them, at least in a parenting capacity, but she'd also made it sound like he was the last man on earth she'd consider. "It's all about wanting what you can't have," he said.

"Did Jack say that?" Priscilla asked.

"No, I did. I think it's what makes Pop tick, and it's a dangerous way to live."

"I'll say." Priscilla topped off their tea. "So back to your deal."

He sighed. "I haven't worked it out fully yet. I'm just thinking you and I might be able to work together pretty well."

"To whose benefit?"

"I haven't figured that out yet, either. It's a work in progress." Pete shoved his hat back, drummed the table with his fingers. "The pieces are slowly coming together for me."

"That's encouraging."

"Yeah." He squinted, considering her for a moment. "There are certain pieces that are eluding me."

"Like?"

"Why'd my father choose you?" He quit drumming, looked at her thoughtfully. Priscilla was a pretty woman, and judging from Gabriel's and Dane's new wives, Pop liked women who were easy on the eyes. Probably thought it boded well for grandchildren, which made sense, Pete supposed. "You have no children, unlike Laura and Suzy. You live nearly two hours away, unlike Laura and Suzy, who were both living in Union Junction. I know my father is a serial matchmaker, yet I just wonder, why you?"

"I…couldn't guess."

"Well, maybe he thought you were the motherly type," Pete theorized.

"He hadn't even met me."

"That's true." Pete shook his head. "I'm confused."

"Does it matter?" Priscilla asked. "You and I both know that a relationship between us for the sake of children—even as wonderful a man as your father may be—isn't workable."

He nodded slowly. "In fact, it's silly."

"I wouldn't call Josiah silly. 'Determined' is the word I'd choose."

But there were plenty of wonderful women in Union Junction, Pete was sure of it. Yet for some reason, Pop had chosen her. He'd been right on the mark with Laura and Suzy. There was something about Priscilla, something worth considering, for Pop to have picked her. Plus, Pete wasn't entirely immune to her, as much as it pained him to wonder just how well his father knew him.

"As I say," he continued, "all the pieces haven't come together yet for me. But they will. Maybe I'll ask Pop what was on his mind."

"Oh, I wouldn't do that," Priscilla said hurriedly. "Likely he simply knew that Suzy and I were great friends and figured I'd fit in well in Union Junction." She gestured around the tea room. "But as I told Josiah, I have a life I love here."

Pete smiled. "Pop didn't offer to move the house and tea shop to Union Junction?"

Priscilla didn't smile. "No."

"Didn't offer you money?"

"Nope. Just children and a husband, none of which were his to wheel and deal for."

"Yeah," Pete said. "But I know why he did it. That part I do understand, or at least I'm beginning to understand." He leaned back, considering her for a moment. "Would you like to go for a drive? I see that sign says your shop is closed on Sundays."

"I might," she said. "Depends on what I'm going to see."

"A surprise," Pete said. "Pack an overnight bag."

"You're taking me to see the babies," she guessed, and he tried to decide whether she sounded nervous about the babies or being with him.

"I thought we might. I don't even know why, except that I'm feeling unsuccessful right now, since Jack took off like a shot out of a cannon when he heard what was on my mind." He scratched under his hat, then shook his head. "Jack had it harder than the rest of us. He never did anything right, as far as Pop was concerned."

Pete looked at Priscilla, seeing that she was listening with sympathy, so he took a deep breath and went on, "The thing about Jack was that he'd give any of us the shirt off his back. Of all of us, Jack was the one who'd come running if we needed a pat on the head, a little encouragement. It kills me to see him so gun-shy now. Pop did that to him."

"Oh, dear," Priscilla said. "I'm so sorry."

Pete waved a hand, trying to appear casual. "I came home all ready to tell Pop what I thought about his letter. All the years of anger were ready to spill right out of me, so I understand Jack's reaction today. I really do. I just hadn't counted on Pop needing us, the jackass. It sort of turns the tables on any bitter words I'd thought about saying to him."

"I think living in the past is pretty hard sometimes," Priscilla said, breaking eye contact. "A lot of regrets back there."

"Yeah. To be honest, I wasn't too happy to find you there at the ranch with him. I'd built up a full head of steam. It'd been simmering inside me since I'd left the States. I was really going to ride the old man." He shrugged. "There was Miss Manners, though, and I had to give Pop a pass in the interest of chivalry."

"Aren't you glad you did?"

He sighed. "Are you coming or not?"

Standing, Priscilla took off her apron. "I happen to be free for the evening."

"Good." He crossed his legs, leaned back in the chair. "That makes two of us."

PRISCILLA DID WANT to see the quadruplets, but she was a wee bit anxious. Pete was a tempting man, and who wouldn't want to help four orphaned infants?

All she could hope was that wonderful homes could be found for them. She could also hope that Pete would head on his merry way to whatever place next caught his fancy so that she could quit thinking about him. He was invading her daydreams on a disturbingly frequent level. Did she want to end up like Cricket, fancying someone she couldn't have?

It didn't take great brain power to know that she and Pete had nothing in common except for their concern for the babies.

"This is the Union Junction hospital, the babies' home for the past few weeks," Pete said, pulling into the parking lot. "I don't know how much longer they'll need to be here, but they don't seem to mind, fortunately."

She quietly followed Pete inside, reassured by his warmth and strength and sense of duty. They rode the elevator to the second floor, then walked to the nursery window. "And there they are," Pete said, "one, two, three and four."

"Oh," Priscilla said faintly, "they're cherubs."

No one could resist such sweet little babies. Their tiny fannies were covered by small diapers. A hospital-issued bracelet encircled each of four impossibly small arms. Adorable caps were on their heads, and each wore a small T-shirt, a blanket half covering them, though one of the girls had kicked her blanket off. All of them slept peacefully, unaware of the two adults staring at them through the nursery window.

He nodded. "Can't believe they're all from one family."

Priscilla could feel tears pricking at her eyes. "They're so helpless." She looked up at Pete. "It's one thing to hear about them, quite another to see them. No wonder your father is so stirred up."

"Yeah. If he was any younger, he'd be finding himself a bride and adopting them himself."

"Let's go," Priscilla said. Her sudden urge to escape was overwhelming. She couldn't bear to think, hated to remember that once long ago she'd put a child up for adoption, a child just as helpless as these. "Pete, I have to get out of here."

She hurried down the stairs as fast as she could, not bothering with the elevator.

"Hey," Pete said, catching her by the hand as he followed her out. "What just happened back there?"

She took deep breaths. "I don't know. I'm not sure."

He pulled her close, patted her back comfortingly. "Ah. Pop's got you freaked out."

"Maybe," she said, but that wasn't it.

"Listen," he said, "I brought you here to make you happy. I think it's fun to see the little cuties. Two boys, two girls, how cool is that? Forget about Pop. He's a schemer, and he will be until the day he dies."

Priscilla allowed herself to relax against Pete's chest. Still, she couldn't shake the painful emotions.

She hadn't allowed herself to think about her youthful indiscretion in years, at least not consciously.

"Priscilla," Pete said, tipping her face up to meet his, "don't be scared." And then he gently kissed her lips, so sweetly and so tenderly that Priscilla knew she had something new to worry about.

"So you liked them," Josiah said with a broad grin. "They're pretty durn irresistible."

"Yes," Pete said as Priscilla sat across from him in his father's study, "and we think we've come up with an idea." He'd talked Priscilla into stopping by the house with him to visit Pop, in spite of the kiss that she seemed shaken by and determined to ignore. He couldn't blame her. He didn't know why he'd done it, other than a sheer, raw desire to connect with her. "We wanted to share our idea with you."

"Let's hear it." Josiah perked up.

"Priscilla and I thought a community-wide garage sale to benefit the babies would be helpful. Then whoever adopts them will already have all the special equipment and everything they need." Pete nodded at his father, grinned at Priscilla. "We don't have all the details yet. It's an idea that's just been brewing since we left the hospital."

"It's a terrible idea!" Josiah exclaimed. "I mean, if they need things, people can just donate them. Hell, I'll donate everything!" He looked at the two of them, crestfallen. "Is that the best you can come up with?"

"I'm sure, given time, we can think of more ideas—"

"They don't have time, son!" Josiah thundered. "They need—" he cast a sneaky glance at Priscilla "—a mother and a father more than they need toys and trinkets."

Priscilla blushed. Pete shook his head, somewhat embarrassed himself but not surprised his father stayed on key. "Pop, moms and dads are in short supply."

"I'll say," Josiah grumbled.

"And that's up to child welfare, likely even the state," Priscilla reminded him. "Even if we applied, there's no guarantee we'd be chosen or that they'd stay together. You know this, Josiah."

He pursed his lips. "Hope springs eternal."

"Maybe," Priscilla said. "Have you considered any other candidates for Pete? That might be your best option."

Both men stared at her.

"Well," Priscilla said reasonably, "I promise not to be jealous if you can find a more willing bride for your son."

"I'll choose my own wife!"

"Oh, good," Josiah said. "Have you got a short list we can work with?"

"So short there's none on it," Pete admitted.

"Well, that was a fast and circular got-us-nowhere." Josiah rubbed his chin. "Priscilla, you mentioned your business is in trouble. I'll write you a check today for the amount you're owing if you marry my son."

"Josiah, Pete and I are not the match you think we'd be."

"I actually don't care," Josiah said, "as long as you both promise to be good parents. Isn't that the point here?"

Pete looked at Priscilla. "I'm so embarrassed for him," he told her. "I really am. He's the only one in the family, I promise. The rest of the tree is pretty sane."

"It's all right." She sighed. "Listen, let's try to put our heads together and think of a practical solution for the children."

"Okay," Josiah said, "but I would think Pete's million dollars is practical enough."

"Oh, am I up for that now?" Pete asked.

"If you can drag *her* to the altar," his father told him, "I'll throw in fifty thousand for her business."

"My business," Priscilla pointed out, "is in Fort Wylie."

"Yes," Josiah said, his gaze turning devious again, "but I think it's time you start a franchise."

Pete and Priscilla stared at the oldest Morgan.

"Franchise what?" Priscilla asked.

"Your tea shop. We need one here," Josiah said. "And I have land. For that matter, I own a building in Union Junction where your tea shop could be located. Wouldn't the ladies love a tea shop in town?"

"Josiah, I think I'd be too busy raising four children to run two shops," Priscilla said. "That is, if I fell in with your plan, which I most certainly will not."

"Woman!" Josiah thundered. "Don't you have a price?"

Pete admired Priscilla's insistence that she could not be bought. He laughed. "Pop, you've met your match."

Josiah shook his head. "Something's not right here. Something's hanging you up," he told Priscilla. "He's not that ugly, you know. Wasn't that bad a kid. Guess he could have been worse." He leaned back in his desk chair. "Either he or Jack might have taken that prize, I suppose."

Pete perked up at that faint praise. "Weren't you going to say that Jack was your worst? Your letter seemed to indicate that."

"Not being competitive, are you?" Josiah demanded.

"It's sort of what you alluded to in your letter to him," Pete said.

Josiah frowned. "No one was supposed to read Jack's letter but Jack."

"You left his and mine unsealed, Pop. Suzy, Priscilla and Cricket found them. That's how Jack and I received ours. What were they doing in a kitchen drawer, anyway?"

"I wasn't finished writing them," Josiah said with a sheepish glance at Priscilla. "Maybe I wasn't certain I'd said exactly what I'd wanted to say."

"Oh," Pete said, "so maybe my letter was supposed to be an ode to a young man who'd made his father proud?"

"Probably not," Josiah said, unfazed by his son's needling. "However, you shouldn't have read Jack's." He swung his gaze to Priscilla. "I suppose you read Jack's, too," he said.

"I most certainly did not!" Priscilla tapped his arm. "You should know better than that."

"I never did understand why you didn't assign me a woman, Pop—not that I was looking. Or am looking," he said to reassure Priscilla. "You hand-picked women for both Gabe and Dane, sent them letters about the women, so you can understand my curiosity." It really bothered him that his letter had solely been one of condemnation. "All I got was criticism."

"You're the second oldest," Josiah said. "I don't have to look out for you as much as your younger brothers."

Hope rose inside Pete. Maybe Pop really was being honest. "Is that true?"

"If you want it to be. However, notice that as soon as I found a good woman for you, I introduced you." He smiled sweetly at Priscilla. "And anyway, a father shows his love by disciplining his children. That's what's wrong with the world today—kids aren't disciplined. Parents are too busy being cool to be parents. Well, I never worried about being a cool friend to you boys—I was a parent, by golly."

Pete shook his head. Priscilla glanced out the window.

"Oh, look! Suzy and Laura are coming to see you, Josiah!"

Josiah sat up, trying to peer out the window. "And they've brought their families. Good. We'll order pizza."

"I invited them," Pete said, opting for honesty. "I think we need to have a family powwow."

Josiah glared at him. "About putting me in an old folks' home?"

"About the babies," Pete said. "Although you're beginning to whine like one. C'mon, Pop, let me help you to your feet so you can greet your visitors."

Pete gently helped his father up. Josiah gave him a pat on the back. "I think you're winning her over," he whispered to Pete.

Pete shook his head. "Hope springs eternal, Pop."

"That's what I told you, son. I'm glad you're finally listening."

"Yeah. My life is just a rerun of *Father Knows Best*," Pete said, winking at Priscilla.

She didn't wink or smile in return. Instead, she shook her head and hurried out the door to greet her friends. Pete had a sudden premonition that his father was right on more than one level. Something *was* hanging that woman up—and he didn't have the first idea what it was.

Chapter Six

Laura and Gabriel sat in the den with their two children. Laura was in the full bloom of pregnancy, due to deliver in May. Gabe was a proud father and a happy husband, that was easy to see. Priscilla enjoyed seeing their happiness. Suzy and Dane, although married only a month, also were clearly in love. Their twin daughters, Sandra and Nicole, were playing with Penny and Perrin, Laura's and Gabe's little girl and boy. Penny, the oldest of the gang, was the clear leader of the group; the other little ones seemed content to follow. Perrin, now seventeen months old, was really too small to play yet, but he did his best to keep up. Josiah's eyes were dancing with joy.

The old man was in his element. If he'd been slow and tired before, the arrival of the children energized him. Priscilla helped Suzy and Laura serve tea and cookies to everyone—although Josiah insisted he should be allowed a beer, they gave him tea, too—

and then they all sat down to hear Pete's reason for calling them together.

"It's come to Pop's attention that there are four orphaned newborns—quadruplets—in the county who need a family," Pete said. "Pop came up with a convoluted plan for Priscilla and I to adopt them—"

This brought whistles from his brothers and laughter from the women. Priscilla could feel her cheeks heat as she shook her head. "Not me," she said. "You two should know me better than that." It was important to say that out loud, to stress her noncompliance with Josiah's machinations so that everyone understood her position—including Pete. She still wasn't certain of what to make of their kiss earlier.

They seemed to be treading on dangerous ground.

"But as you can tell, Priscilla and I don't think Pop's plan is entirely workable," Pete continued to general laughter. Priscilla's reluctance had been noted.

"We think it might be difficult to convince child services that an ex-military man with no employment at the moment, and a woman who lives nearly two hours away should suddenly team up and be appropriate parents for the babies." Pete looked around at his family. "And yet, we do think we have the blessing of resources in the Morgan clan."

"That's true," Gabe said, "but they'll need more than that."

"And yet it's a start," Pete said. "More importantly, beyond money, they need one family."

Everyone stared at him silently.

"You're the only one who doesn't already have a family, bro," Dane said. "Now, I'm willing to help, but I'm still trying to figure out how to be the best father to the twins."

"Ah," Josiah said on a groan, "think about you four when you were young. You weren't that much trouble, were you?"

"You said we were," Pete reminded him. "Although everybody in this town knows you were a pretty tough taskmaster, Pop."

"All the more reason you could probably sway the adoption agency to consider you, son," Josiah said equitably. "I'm sure my reputation precedes me. Honesty, fairness, generosity, excellent fathering skills…and with them knowing I'd be keeping a firm eye on my sons' parenting duties, those children would have more than most."

Priscilla wasn't sure Josiah was selling his memory of his sons' childhood quite the way they remembered it. They all wore pained grimaces, expressions that tickled Suzy and Laura.

"You turned out fairly well, honey," Laura told Gabe.

He enjoyed the compliment but wasn't about to credit his father.

"You're a catch," Suzy told Dane. "I like you well enough, at least for the month I've been married to you. The jury is still out in some respects, but—"

"But you're crazy about me," Dane said, stealing a kiss.

It was all so easy, Priscilla realized. The two couples had an ease with each other that she and Pete simply didn't have. She seemed to grow more uncomfortable around him all the time. Being a part of this gathering didn't feel like a natural fit, either. Even though Josiah liked her, she knew she would never fit in the way he wanted her to.

She would never be a part of this happy family.

Suddenly she wanted to go home. It would be rude to say so, so she busied herself in the kitchen and played with the children while everyone talked in the den. She could still hear them in the other room.

"Let's think about it some more," Pete said. "I'm sure there's something we can do to help. I just haven't hit the right idea yet."

"It'll come to us," Gabe said. "I, too, hate to think of those kids being broken up."

Josiah beamed at his sons. "You make me proud," he said, and the whole room went silent.

"Oh, hell, don't act like I never said the words before," Josiah said. "What a bunch of emotionally needy weenies I raised. Priscilla! I'll have my afternoon toddy now. I need it to hang with this herd of emotional lightweights."

"I'll get it," Pete said quickly. "Pop, you can't just bellow at Priscilla like she's family."

Everyone went silent again. Priscilla hesitated.

"I mean, Pop, look." Pete sighed. "This bride-picking thing—Priscilla and I are friends. You can't just assume she wants to be part of our family and expect her to wait on you hand and foot."

"I think I know something about women, son," Josiah said, "and what I know is that they're happiest when they're married and having children. Your mother's happiest days were when she was having babies. All women probably secretly dream of being good wives and mothers."

The women's jaws dropped. The men seemed stunned, not knowing what to say to their father.

"Well, they are," Josiah said defensively. "Aren't you happy, Laura? Suzy?"

The women remained silent, staring at Josiah, amazed by his audacity.

Josiah sniffed, not liking that he somehow wasn't being recognized as the authority on what women wanted and what they didn't. "If you're implying I'm a male chauvinist, I most certainly am not. I've always treated women with enormous respect."

"Actually," Priscilla said from the den's entranceway, "I'd love to get married if I were a different woman. But the truth is, I like my life just as it is. I'm happy with what I've done for myself. And I'll get Josiah his toddy, not because I think he's being chauvinistic, but because I know how to fix it better than Pete does." Priscilla walked back into the kitchen, telling herself she was being completely honest about her views on marriage—when deep inside, she knew she wasn't.

Not entirely.

PETE DROVE Priscilla back to Fort Wylie that evening. She'd been quiet, and Pete figured her mood was appropriate. His family was pretty boisterous, as far as an outsider would see it. Plus, Pop treated her like she was his personal servant, calling on her to attend to him every now and again. Maybe he just wanted reassurance that she was still around, and he was trying to show her that he was a fairly harmless old man.

She'd become more withdrawn as the evening progressed. He and his brothers and their wives had kicked around all kinds of ideas for the care of the quadruplets—none of them seemed right, though. Through it all, Josiah had listened, his eyes keen with interest.

Pete still felt as if he was part of a grand scheme— he wondered if Priscilla felt the same. It was a long drive and neither of them had a lot to say. They talked about the weather, how this February was a particularly cold month. They discussed small matters, avoiding the subjects of children, matrimony and family. It was pretty tricky navigating, considering that children, matrimony and family was all that his family had talked about.

He didn't expect her to invite him in, but when they arrived at her house, she turned and said, "Can you come in for a few moments?"

"Are you sure you're not too tired for company?"

She shook her head. "I'm not tired. In fact, you could probably use a break from driving. And there's something I'd like to discuss with you."

This sounded reasonable to Pete, so he parked his truck and followed her into her cozy home. As cute as the tea parlor was, the part of the structure that was her home was warmly welcoming. He could see why she'd never want to leave her house.

She brought out tea and cookies from the kitchen, setting them on a coffee table before gesturing him to find a place to sit. "Make yourself comfortable, Pete."

He'd be more comfortable if he knew why he'd been asked in. During the drive she'd had two hours to talk to him, yet there was something more she felt she had to say? He munched a cookie and waited for her to lead the discussion.

"Why did you kiss me?" she asked.

Cookie crumbs got caught in his throat at his sudden inhalation. After he stopped choking, he looked at her with watery eyes. "Sorry. Went down the wrong pipe." He hoped that would make her forget her question, but she sat waiting, her eyes wide as she waited for his answer.

"I kissed you," he said, "because I wanted to."

She didn't say a word.

"Was there a problem?" he asked, and she shook her head.

"No."

What was a guy supposed to make of that? Had she liked it or not? She wasn't about to give him any clues, however, so he just sat there, waiting.

Finally he couldn't stand it any longer. "Do you want me to kiss you again?"

"Not tonight," she said, "and after I tell you this, you may never *want* to again."

"Uh-oh," he said, "if you're about to make some kind of confession, I'm not the one to hear it."

"It is a confession," she said softly, her eyes downcast.

"You know, I'm not good with emotional stuff," Pete said. "Since I've been home I've been trying to connect with my father and my brothers, make up for lost time. It's only been a few days. All this baby conversation, marriage stuff—it's not easy for me. I've been on my own a long time. Being in the military kind of teaches you to rely on yourself. Please don't confess anything to me, because I'm worse than Pop when it comes to being a male chauvinist. I really think I am."

He was aware he was running, heading away from deep water as fast as he could. He hoped she'd let him get away with it. He'd never been a pillow-talk kind of man—she probably had that figured out.

"I know these little orphans are very much on your family's mind," Priscilla said, "and I wish I could help. Short of a bake sale or something, I can't. In fact, the whole topic is a bit painful to me. I know children make your father stronger," she told him, her voice soft. "Anyone can see he draws his strength from family, but…I gave a child up for adoption when I was seventeen."

He stared at her. She didn't cry, wasn't saying the words looking for sympathy. It was a straightforward statement of fact. "I'm sorry," he said, truly feeling that way but not knowing if those were the words she needed to hear.

"I am, too," she said, in that same flat tone. "All the discussion of adopting has brought the past back to me in a very personal way." She swallowed and he thought she might cry, but she looked him in the eye and went on, "Adopting children when I gave one up would be impossible for me. I would feel as if…I didn't deserve them. I don't know how else to explain it."

He crossed the room to sit beside her on the sofa. "Priscilla, I'm sorry my family has put you in this position. Frankly none of us had the right to drag you into our personal issues. We're a little selfish that way." He took a deep breath. "You're a wonderful woman, and my father likes you, that's why he's trying so hard to figure out a way to move you into the family. By no means are you obligated to do so. Believe me, Pop's last intention is for you to feel awkward. He just wants you around. I figured that out tonight when he kept trying to get you to look after him."

She smiled. "I didn't mind."

"He's up to his old tricks, although I thought he'd

decided I wasn't worth his time. This is habitual family-making for Pop, so please don't think any more of it. The last thing any of us meant to do was make you feel uncomfortable."

She looked at him a long time, then slowly nodded. "Okay."

To take the edge off the awkwardness, he said, "Is it a bad time to ask you for that kiss?"

He hoped she'd smile, but she didn't. She simply leaned forward and placed her lips against his, giving him a brief kiss.

He wasn't sure if he was forgiven or getting the boot. "Are we friends now?" he asked.

"I'm not sure," she said.

"Give a guy a little direction," he told her, wanting desperately to kiss her senseless but not certain if he'd just been given a kiss-off.

"It was nothing," she told him, and his heart crumpled a little. "Just my way of saying that I'm sorry I can't be what you need."

"Oh, hell," he said, "I don't know what I need."

A small smile lifted her lips. "Your father will find you a wife to help you adopt those babies."

"I wish that wasn't true, but it's sort of like wishing the wind won't blow." He looked at Priscilla again, realizing she really was trying to let him down gently. "I guess I'll put on my hat and go."

"All right." She stood, and he followed suit, finally getting the direction he'd asked for.

"Hey, don't be a stranger," he told her. "We're really pretty harmless at the Morgan ranch."

She walked him to the door. "Depends on the definition of 'harmless.' Good night, Pete."

"Good night." He touched her cheek, a gentle caress that wouldn't cross any boundaries, and headed out into the cold.

Chapter Seven

Pete had done a lot of soul-searching. He'd prayed a lot and consulted his brothers about the four babies in the Union Junction hospital. In the end, he'd realized he couldn't leave these children behind. He had a chance to make up for some of the children he hadn't been able to save in his job as an agent. This adoption would cleanse his soul in a way, and give him a purpose in life. Being a father, he'd realized all of a sudden like an unbidden beam of light, was his calling. His chance at redemption in his own life, and frankly, with his own family.

So now he sat in a small, organized office, staring into the face of a compact, efficient woman who didn't seem impressed that he was there to perform a rescue.

"There's a lot of paperwork involved in adoptions, I'm sure you're aware of that," Mira Gaines, head of the child-welfare services in Union Junction, said. "These children are already wards of the state, as they have no living relatives. Mr. Morgan, while I respect your desire to see that the children are cared for, I can't help wondering why a single man would want to adopt four infants."

She blinked at him from behind black glasses, and Pete knew he hadn't gotten a gold star on his request yet. "I was raised with three brothers. We were pretty close. It's not like I don't know what goes into raising a big family."

"True enough. But these are special-needs infants at this time," she explained. "You'd need a lot of help."

"Which I'm fortunate enough to have right here in Union Junction, as well as the financial resources required to raise four kids." He didn't, not yet, but he knew Pop would be a more than doting grandfather. The children wouldn't lack for anything. "You should at least consider me," he said.

"Of course you'll be considered. All applicants are."

"Have there been any others?"

"This isn't a town raffle, Mr. Morgan. The children will be put into a national registry where families who have been, frankly, on waiting lists for years can be matched to their needs."

"They'll be broken up," he said glumly, fear washing over him. "Do you understand how hard that would be on a family?"

"They're very young," she said.

"You're implying that they won't remember. That they'll be loved by their new families and won't ever know what they lost."

"We do the best we can, Mr. Morgan," she said gently. "Life isn't perfect. If it was, the children would still have their own parents."

He shook his head, frustrated with the situation.

"The fact is, it's not up to me," she said, her voice still gentle. "Their cases will be reviewed by a state board. It's very difficult for everyone, and all parties involved will do their best to make the most important decision of these young childrens' lives. Your application would be considered, but I have to be honest—it's a serious long shot."

"It would be better if I was married," he said flatly.

"Of course a married couple will be looked on more favorably, but it's not the end of the discussion. If you're determined and still want to do this, we can certainly begin the process."

His lips twisted. "I may as well. We have the space at the ranch."

Mrs. Gaines looked at him sympathetically. "I understand your father hasn't been well. Are you certain he wants babies in his home? They do tend to cry often in the night, you know, times four. The noise level would go up dramatically, as well as the activity."

He stood. "Believe me when I tell you that my father would think their crying was the sound of angels singing."

She considered Pete for a long time. He sat very

still, keeping his face impassive, knowing he was under the most intense scrutiny of his life.

Mrs. Gaines finally gave a small nod. "Let's get started with the initial paperwork, then."

THAT NIGHT Pete had to admit to his father that going it alone as an adoptive father didn't seem likely. "They didn't give me a whole lot of hope," he told his father, noticing Josiah's disappointment. Pop looked more tired with each passing day, he realized. It wasn't just the long journey home from France that had worn him down—his father simply wasn't in the best of health. "Have you talked to your doctor here in town since you've been back?"

"Son, I've seen doctors here and in France. I've taken the waters. I've sat in miracle chairs overseen by praying nuns. Believe me, I've tried everything. Fact is, I've lived a longer and better life than most, so I'm accepting it." He eyed his son sharply. "Stay on the point."

"I am," Pete said with a sigh. "A one-to-four ratio isn't good as far as child-welfare services is concerned. The general feeling seems to be that I don't know what I'm asking for. I don't think I've got a prayer."

"Where's Priscilla, anyway?" Josiah asked.

"Back in her home and tea shop." Pete waved a hand. "Don't count her into the picture, Pop."

"Durn," Josiah said, "I like her."

"I know. But we don't always get to have what we like."

His father sighed. "You talk to me like I'm a baby. At least she respects me."

Pete laughed. "Pop, I do respect you."

"Better than you used to, anyhow." Josiah rearranged his blanket over his legs. "Throw another log on the fire, will you?"

Pete did as his father requested, watching the sparks fly. "Maybe they're right. Maybe we couldn't handle four children."

Pop grunted. "If anybody can, we can."

"Yeah, but we pretty much ran amok as kids, Pop, face it."

"No, you took care of each other. That's why you're all reasonably strong. Although you could be stronger. Occasionally you can all be a bit wishy-washy, but you're coming along. Slowly."

Pete had to laugh, no longer bothered by Pop's incessant carping, recognizing it as a form of teasing. "Slow and steady wins the race."

"Yeah, well. Where there's a will, there's a will. We'll just have to test a few different plans," Josiah said with a gleam in his eye.

THE NEXT NIGHT Pete learned what kind of "different plans" his father had in mind. In the living room sat six women, all dressed as if they were going to church, except for one who wore a nurse's uniform.

All the women were smiling at him like he was some sort of prize. Josiah was the center of attention, clearly enjoying all this female company. "Hello, everyone," Pete said cautiously, taking off his hat and setting it on a nearby chair.

All the women said hello, followed by some nervous giggles. That alone had Pete's antennae quivering. "What's up, Pop?" He hadn't showered; he'd been out looking at some heifers, thinking about what he wanted to do now that he was a free man. He thought about ranching, which would probably make Pop happy. He'd considered breeding horses. There were a lot of opportunities he wanted to research, and the last thing he wanted was a room full of anxious women.

"Just having a little gathering," Pop said jovially. "These nice ladies came over to check on me."

Since the women were closer to Pete's age than his father's, Pete doubted the statement. "Excellent. Then I'll just head upstairs and leave you to your party."

"No, no!" Josiah exclaimed, his tone a trifle too jovial. "Come join us. Ladies, this is my second son, Pete."

There was another round of hellos. Pete shifted, beginning to realize his first instinct had been correct— Pop was up to no good. Pete was trapped. He couldn't abruptly leave without seeming rude. So he sat.

He met Marty Carroll, who was in residency for her medical degree. She planned to be a pediatrician.

With pretty blue eyes and a soft voice, Pete felt certain Dr. Carroll would be very comforting to babies.

He met Judy Findley, a dietician at Union Junction's hospital. Dark-haired and petite with a sweet smile, Pete knew dinner would always be nutritious—and four little babies would never drink soda.

He met Susan Myer, a generously curved, pretty librarian. Pete knew four little babies would have the benefit of constantly being read wonderful books.

He met Crissy Cates, a tall, red-haired nurse with a no-nonsense demeanor but a genial laugh. Pete knew four little babies would always have practical caregiving advice at hand.

He met Zoe Pettigrew, a tiny, thin church secretary with the sexiest eyes he'd ever seen on a church secretary. Pete figured Pop was counting on Zoe to drag four little babies to church often.

Last he met Chara Peppertree, a beautiful model type, with brown eyes, long brown hair and long fingernails that were painted red. Pete glanced at Pop curiously, but Pop just shrugged. Then Chara said, "It's a pleasure to meet you, Pete" in a lovely voice, and Pete understood that four little babies would always have beauty around them.

Pete had no idea what to do with so much delightful feminine attention—except he couldn't help thinking it was Priscilla who made his heart race. She had from the moment he'd met her. Right now, his heart wasn't racing with anything more than a healthy desire to roar at his father for being such a manipulative old codger.

But Priscilla wasn't here—and she wasn't even available, as she'd pointed out—so Pete sat down and let himself be courted. After all, there were four little babies to think about. And these days, they were heavily on Pete's mind.

"COME WITH ME, Cricket," Priscilla said as she packed an overnight bag while Cricket sat on her bed and watched.

"Well, I wouldn't mind seeing the Morgans again, and I could use a weekend away." Cricket winked at Priscilla. "Besides, I don't mind seeing how you're going to present this plan to Pete."

"I wouldn't go if Laura and Suzy hadn't invited me out for the party." Priscilla finished packing her suitcase. "They wanted you to come along, if you could."

"Laura and Suzy invited me, too?"

Priscilla nodded and closed the case. "Suzy's exact words were 'You might want to come out. Josiah's having a matchmaking party. Bring Cricket for backup.'"

Cricket smiled. "An old-fashioned matchmaking party. Josiah's fun, isn't he?"

"I don't know," Priscilla said honestly. "I'm not the woman for Pete, I know that. Still, I think about him all the time." She shrugged. "I've gone over it so many times in my head that just when I'm proud of myself for being practical, I feel dumb for possibly passing up the one man I feel something for."

"Wow, that's a dilemma," Cricket said. "I wish I had it."

Priscilla looked at her friend. "You have a dilemma and its name is Jack, which is the real reason you're coming along with me."

"Not true," Cricket said airily. "The chance of him ever showing up at the ranch is zero. Plus, to be honest, it's best if I don't entertain that particular dead end."

"True," Priscilla said. "The same goes for me."

"Yet a matchmaking party sounds kind of fun," Cricket said with a giggle. "I hope you're the guest of honor."

Priscilla smiled. "Sometimes I almost do feel part of the family."

Chapter Eight

Pete was exhausted by nine o'clock. Talking to women was a sport in which he might be out of practice, he decided as the women said their goodbyes. He escorted all of them to their cars, thanked them for coming and went inside to grab a beer and have a word with Pop.

Josiah grinned at him when he walked in the door. "Fun stuff, eh?"

"Not so much. Please don't ever do that again on my behalf." He flung himself onto the sofa.

"Didn't you have fun?"

"I did. But I'd have had just as much fun watching TV."

Pop laughed. "Methinks you doth protest too much. But that's okay."

Pete shook his head, knowing his father wouldn't be deterred easily from his path. "I didn't fail to notice that all those women had sterling occupations for adoption applications. Nurse, pediatrician, et cetera, et cetera. Although the model threw me."

"Ah, well. A man's gotta have something really glamorous to look at every once in a while. She sort of reminded me of your mother with all that dark-eyed beauty."

Pete sat up. "Pop, why don't you call Mom? All you ever do is talk about her."

"Why don't you call her? She's your mother."

Pete blinked. Rubbed his face, scratched his head, stared at his father. "She left. Figured she didn't want to hear from us."

Josiah nodded. "Well, don't act like I've been keeping you from something you want to do."

"I never said you were." Pete frowned, trying to remember why, if it was as easy as picking up a phone, he'd never spoken to his mother. "Did we have a telephone when we were growing up?"

"Well, we did, sort of," Pop said. "There wasn't a phone for years, of course, because the poles didn't get put in out this way for a long time. Part of the price of country living. Then we had this thing where you dialed up and asked an operator to put the call through. Of course we had a party line, and it was hell waiting on a chance to get a call through. There was no such thing, of course, as a transatlantic call, not out here. Maybe in the big city." He glanced at his son. "'Course nowadays, calling around the world is nothing difficult."

Nothing difficult, said his world-traveling father.

"Guess I'll turn in," Pop said. "You're boring after all the pretty ladies we had here."

The doorbell rang, and Pop perked up. "Perhaps a straggler," he said, his hopes high. "Maybe one of those gals was taken with you and is trying to get an early jump on her rivals. Let's go see."

"Sure, Pop," Pete said, putting up with the teasing with good humor, until he opened the door and saw Cricket and Priscilla standing on the porch.

"We heard there was a party," Priscilla said, her smile a little shy. "Suzy said we should come." She glanced over her shoulder. "But I don't see any cars. Do we have the wrong time?"

Josiah grinned at Pete, not ruffled at all by his daughter-in-law's interference. "That Suzy has such true Morgan spirit."

Priscilla's gaze searched Pete's. "She said it was a matchmaking party. We have no idea what that is, but it sounded like fun, and since she invited us, we thought we could at least help out."

Josiah ushered them inside. "We love any kind of gathering around here."

Cricket glanced around. "Did we miss the party?" she asked, eyeing the desserts, which were still on the dining-room table.

"It wasn't much of a party," Pete said. "Help yourself to some snacks."

"By all means," Josiah said, "and if you'll excuse

me, I think I'll retire to the TV room. Cricket, you can join me if you like."

Cricket looked at Pete. "He's not very subtle, is he?"

Pete shook his head. "'Subtle' is not a word that's used to describe Pop."

Cricket followed Josiah from the room after filling a paper plate with some treats. Priscilla looked at Pete. "What just happened here?"

Pete had a feeling these women, too, were victims of Pop's good intentions. "Have a seat," he said. "The story's not your typical boy-meets-girl."

"Sounds interesting."

He was glad to see her. Priscilla gave him a feeling none of the other women who'd visited had. "It's always interesting with Pop. He threw me a lady shower."

She raised a brow. "Oh, how nice for you."

"It was." She frowned at him, and he reconsidered his words. "I mean, it was nice that Pop did that for me, but talking to a bunch of women is taxing."

"Oh, I'm *sure*."

She didn't sound sure. "It is," he told her. "How much can a guy say to women he doesn't know?"

"I have no idea. But I bet you gave it your best effort."

He looked at her. She didn't sound jealous—and part of him sort of hoped she would be.

"So he's moved on from me and looking for a new candidate?" Priscilla asked.

"I suppose so. You know, I didn't ask Pop what the plan had been. I just asked him not to do it again."

"You did?"

"Yes." He nodded, hoping she believed him. "I used to wonder why he hadn't found me a bride. Not that I wanted one, of course. But I'd wondered if he didn't deem me as worthy of a wife as my brothers. Maybe he didn't see the same potential in me as a good husband, good father, good son. But since he learned about the babies, he's gone into overdrive. I'm merely a pawn in this game of achieving his greater goal."

She smiled. "I think he loves you very much. It's nice when parents are concerned about their children."

"It's a new phase in our relationship." He thought it was a topic best left alone and tried to change the subject. "So, pretty cold outside, huh?"

"I'd say it's normal for February." Priscilla helped herself to a sugar cookie. "So Suzy tried to pull a fast one on your father by inviting me."

"Pop was amused by it," Pete said.

"I feel a bit awkward."

"Don't," he said, meaning it.

"What if we'd shown up when the party was still in full swing?"

He smiled at her. "You would have swung with the rest of us."

She put the plate on the table. "I shouldn't have come." Standing, she grabbed her purse. Pete realized she was about to make a run for the door and slipped his hand over her wrist.

"Hey," he said, "if you leave, I'll be stuck here with a bunch of desserts I can't eat."

"I really must go. I feel like a party crasher."

He tried to be reassuring. "My father has theories, you know, but they have nothing to do with anything other than his own grandiose plans. I am my own man."

"Josiah reminds me of the king in Cinderella who brought all the beautiful single noblewomen to the castle so his son could choose a bride from among them."

Pete blinked. "Wasn't that a French fairy tale? Pop's just returned from France. He was probably sitting over there swilling the happily-ever-after wine."

"So tonight you were the prince," Priscilla said, and Pete glanced around him.

"See any glass slippers lying around? Shoes of any kind?" he asked.

"Just your boots." Priscilla sat back down. "Maybe I will have a piece of cake."

"I'VE FIGURED OUT a way to save my business," Priscilla told Cricket as they drove back to Fort Wylie a few hours later. She could feel Cricket's curious glance on her, despite the darkness of the surrounding countryside. Occasional lights from oncoming traffic on the two-lane road bounced into the car.

The bitter cold at this hour—nearly midnight—was enough to make a girl shiver. "I need a partner."

"Named Pete Morgan?"

"No!" Priscilla shook her head. "It's a bad idea to mix finances and friendship. I was thinking more of asking you to go into business with me."

"You just said it was a bad idea to mix finance and friendship," Cricket pointed out.

"Among people who have kissed," Priscilla explained. "Then it is a bad idea, I'm sure of it."

"I don't think you mentioned any kissing to me."

"Well," Priscilla said, turning onto the highway outside of Union Junction, "it was so brief I wasn't certain of the meaning."

"I hate those," Cricket said. "I prefer big, juicy smackeroos. Not that I've had any of those lately, but that's what I want when I get one."

"Well," Priscilla said, "I would have been totally shocked if that had happened between Pete and me. It was totally genteel and respectable and possibly a bit boring. Is that my cell phone ringing?"

"I think so. Do you want me to look?"

"Can you? I don't want to scramble for my phone while I'm driving. I can't imagine who'd be calling me at this hour." It was well past the time she'd normally be getting phone calls. She thought of her parents, hoping everything was all right. "Will you answer it for me? If it's Mom, tell her I'm driving and see if everything's okay at home, please."

"Hello?" Cricket said into Priscilla's phone. "Yes, this is Cricket. She's driving right now. Can I give her a message, Pete?" She listened for a minute. "He just wants to thank us for coming out, and asks you to drive safely." Cricket covered the phone. "What do you want me to say?"

Priscilla's heart warmed at the kind words. "Thank you?"

"Lame, but okay." Cricket uncovered the phone. "She says she had a wonderful time, and when's the next matchmaking party?"

Priscilla gasped. "Cricket!"

Cricket covered the phone again. "What? I'm a deacon. No one ever tells the deacon to mind their own business." She held the phone to Priscilla's ear. "He wants to tell you something."

Priscilla listened.

"Hey," Pete said.

"Hi," Priscilla answered.

"You're not upset or anything, are you?"

"Why should I be?" Priscilla wouldn't have admitted it in a million years. A tiny sliver of jealousy had needled her heart at the thought of all those women casting their lures for Pete, but she wasn't the right woman for him, was she? She could be his friend, and only his friend.

"I just wondered," Pete said, "since Cricket asked about another party."

"She likes cake," Priscilla told him, "and she likes to visit your father."

He sighed. "It was easier when my father was a visitor, instead of a permanent resident."

Priscilla smiled. "We did have a lot of fun last month while he was in France. But your dad is fun, too."

"I'm going to get drapes in that house eventually," Cricket said, joining the conversation, though not removing the phone from Priscilla's ear.

"I just want to know," Pete said, "if I adopt the babies by myself, will you completely run away from me?"

"No," Priscilla said slowly, knowing why he was asking, "but I wouldn't make a good stand-in mom, you know."

"I know. I mean, I know that's how you feel. Anyway, thanks for coming out."

"Uninvited," Priscilla said. "Which I plan to discuss with Suzy, by the way."

"Don't," Pete said. "You were the bright spot of my evening." He said goodbye and hung up, leaving Priscilla just as surprised as when he'd unexpectedly kissed her.

"You can turn off the phone," Priscilla told Cricket. "Thanks for holding it so long."

"What happened?" Cricket demanded. "Did you leave a shoe? Does he plan to climb your tower? Does he want to wake you up with a kiss? It's just after midnight—something has to be happening!"

Priscilla laughed. "This is no fairy tale."

"Well?"

"Well," Priscilla said, "I have no idea what that was all about. I think it was a general drive-safely call, along with some flattery."

"Ah, flattery," Cricket said with satisfaction. "Princes are good conversationalists."

"Not usually," Priscilla said. "They usually just show up for the kiss."

"Okay." Cricket put the cell phone back in Priscilla's purse. "You've got a prince who likes to gab."

That was true. And he was talking himself straight into her heart, Priscilla realized. "I think I'd rather have one who just kisses."

"Talking's important."

But Priscilla was pretty certain she and Pete had already said everything that needed to be said—and both of them knew the ending.

"Would you have gone if you'd known Mr. Morgan was having a party to introduce Pete to the local ladies?"

"No! That was embarrassing." Priscilla smiled. "Though we're just friends, it was still awkward."

"I think there's more there than friendship," Cricket said, "but you're going to have to consider the competition now and either dance or get off the floor."

"It would seem grim, if I was interested in Pete, which I'm not. We've discussed this, Pete and I. And he understands why I'm not available for the bride hunt."

"Does he?"

She could feel Cricket's gaze on her. "Of course. Hence the party tonight."

"Should I remind you how handsome he is? What a gentleman he is? That most women would jump at the chance to date him?"

"It's okay," Priscilla said. "There'll be other fish in my sea."

"All right," Cricket said, "but a good fisher-woman would keep her hook baited if such a big catch was in sight."

Priscilla blinked. "Trust me, I do not have the right bait for this catch. Moving on to you, do you have your hook baited in case a great catch swims your way?"

"I don't have the right bait, either," Cricket said with a sigh. "This is a problem we're going to have to work on. Or we can rename your tea shop the House of Old Maids when I go into business with you."

Priscilla perked up. "Really?"

"I think so," Cricket said. "I like the idea of a second business wherein I'm a silent partner. Although I'll probably gain weight because I'll eat my proceeds."

Priscilla smiled. "We'll change the name of it to include you."

"Two Spinsters Tea Shop and Etiquette Lessons?"

"No," Priscilla said with a shake of her head. "We're not spinsters. We're independent women."

"So we'll be the Two Independent Women Tea Shop? Not very catchy, is it?"

Priscilla smiled. "How about Two Friends Tea Shop?"

Cricket nodded. "I like it. The only question I have is, are you deliberately building up your life and putting down more roots in Fort Wylie in order to avoid a certain hunky guy?"

WHEN PETE HUNG UP the phone after speaking to Priscilla, the answer to his dilemma with Priscilla hit him like a thunderbolt. His father was right—something was bothering her. As she'd admitted, at seventeen she'd been pregnant and given away a child. In fairness to the memory of that child, she didn't feel she could create another family.

But if she knew that child was all right, living well and happy, maybe she could move past the guilt and pain to which she'd tied herself. He didn't know for sure, but he'd want to know that any child he'd had was happy and loved. Kids deserved happy childhoods. He wanted to adopt the babies, but the picture he had in his mind was that Priscilla would be part of his life, as well.

Darn Pop for putting that idea in his mind. It was a pretty clear picture, too, one he saw more clearly every day.

The only way to help Priscilla move forward was to ease the past. It wouldn't be all that hard to find out what happened to one little child.

She believed she wasn't cut out to adopt those

children, but he knew she was. She was so soft, so gentle-natured, there was no possible way she wouldn't make a wonderful mother. She insisted her tea shop was all she needed. Yet his father's words gave him pause. Josiah believed Priscilla was the kind of woman who kept her emotions hidden, kept her pain close to her heart. Pete was pretty familiar with emotional scars—he could feel his own starting to fade.

He hadn't brought up the subject of adoption again, but the whole idea of her joining him in the crazy scheme was stuck in his mind. He wanted her to feel good about the quadruplets. They needed love and nurturing, something he knew he could provide, things he knew Priscilla could, too.

But maybe he was wrong about her. Maybe she didn't have the capacity for loving children not of her own body.

THE NEXT AFTERNOON, at his daily self-appointed time, Pete stared through the glass at the babies in the nursery, wondering if he'd ever be able to touch them, hold them, name them something other than Wright 1, 2, 3 and 4. He was pretty sure they needed names; their parents had probably thought of names for them. It didn't seem fair that the babies wouldn't have the names their parents had chosen. Pete closed his eyes for a moment, telling himself that for a spy, he'd certainly turned into a sentimental slob. These babies didn't care what their names were. They cared about food and being comforted when they cried. They were intent on getting through each day, something Pete could relate to. He supposed during his darkest times, when he'd been completely focused on nothing other than survival, not getting caught, refusal to get beaten down by the enemy, he had not cared about his name, either. It hadn't done him any good.

Or maybe it had. Being a Morgan had put steel in his spine and a cage of fearlessness around his brain. He'd been robotlike in his desire to survive. Water, food, shelter—those had been his goals. In the back of his mind, it was Pop who had driven him.

Like Pop was driven now to survive. Pete understood the old man better than he wanted to.

He wished he understood Priscilla, as well. For all that he thought they might be good for each other, she had more defenses than he.

It was somewhat annoying to meet a woman who was his spiritual twin. And yet, he admired her dedication to her own emotional survival.

"Excuse me," he said to the nurse on duty when she left the nursery, "when can I hold them?"

"Mr. Morgan," she said with a smile, "you ask us every day. And every day you know we must tell you the same thing. You probably won't get to hold them, unless your adoption request is approved."

Her brown eyes said that was probably unlikely. "Hey," he said, "kiss them good-night for me, okay?"

"Mr. Morgan," she said, even more gently, "we

don't kiss the babies because we don't want to spread germs to them while they're in a fragile stage of their development. We stroke them and we talk to them, but we don't kiss them, no matter how much we want to."

"You should," he said gruffly. "*I* would."

She nodded. "I know."

She patted him on the back. He barely noticed, and he didn't notice when she left. His attention caught by four little people bent on their own survival, he prayed with all his heart that the babies felt their parents' spirits urging them on.

Chapter Nine

The following week Pete received a visit he never dreamed he'd get. Jack appeared at his side at the nursery window while Pete contemplated the day when—and if—he could ever hold the children in his arms.

"Hi," he heard his brother say.

Pete jumped, shaken from his reverie by the last person he'd expected to see. "What are you doing here?"

Jack shrugged. "Same thing you are, I guess."

Pete stared at his brother. "No. You are not here to look at babies. And you're not here to see me because you wouldn't have known I was here. So what's up?" He was riveted by his brother's genie-like arrival.

"I knew you'd be here," Jack said. "It's common knowledge in town that you're here every day."

"I doubt my comings and goings are of interest to anyone." Pete squinted at his brother. "And you and I have very few people in common who would know my schedule. So what gives?"

"Priscilla said it would be easier to find you here than anywhere."

An arrow of jealousy shot through Pete. "When did you see Priscilla?"

Jack shrugged again. "Had a hankering for cookies and tea, so I stopped by to see her."

Cookies and tea were not the typical fare of the average, down-on-his-luck rodeo cowboy. "Are you going to tell me what's going on, or do I have to beat it out of you?"

The words were the comforting brother-to-brother warfare from their younger years, and Jack grinned. "You and what army?"

"Actually, I'm retired from active duty, so I won't be bringing an army," Pete said gruffly. "How about you just cut to the chase?"

"All right." Jack sighed. "Do we talk here or somewhere else?" he asked with a glance at the babies.

"This is my visiting hour," Pete said. "I can't leave for another five minutes. I'm here every day, and the babies might be upset if I leave. It would change their routine, and it would change mine."

Jack didn't bother to remind him that the babies had no idea who he was. Their world consisted of the kind, gentle hands of the hospital staff who nurtured them. Obviously Pete liked to think they felt his presence.

"Fine. I heard your girlfriend's parents are in a spot of financial trouble. Don't ask me how. I'm just a purveyor of possibly useful information."

"Wait," Pete said, before his brother could lope off, because that was what Jack usually did—appear and disappear within seconds—"do you mean Priscilla?"

"Is she not your girlfriend?" Jack asked quizzically. "Maybe I'm putting my nose in where it doesn't belong, and I really make it a habit not to do that."

If Jack had come to tell him something about Priscilla, then it was something he knew for certain. "Priscilla is a friend. She probably wouldn't want to be called my girlfriend," Pete said, and Jack nodded.

"Too bad about that. She's cute. I thought Pop had probably fixed you up with her."

"Well, he tried." Pete frowned. "But we're not in the same place in life. Anyway, what about her parents?"

"The reason Priscilla's bank loan was reduced dramatically is because her parents co-signed for her business."

"This is getting into the field of none-of-my-business," Pete said, "but how do you know this?"

"One of the women who works with some members of the rodeo-finance committee mentioned that the Perkinses were having financial difficulties. The name caught my attention, because I had met Priscilla. I asked a few more questions and got the answers. Nothing that won't come out in the local newspapers, but I just thought you should know before it becomes general knowledge." Jack paused, then, "Everyone's heard you're trying to adopt these children. I think you're nuts, and obviously Pop's gotten to you, but whatever. As I say, I'm just an anonymous conductor of trivial information."

He started to turn away, preparing to leave. Pete's hand shot out, nabbing his brother. "Wait," he said, "I'll spring for a beer and a steak if you hang around and let me get this sorted out in my mind."

"You're that slow?" Jack asked. "I always thought you were supposed to be the smart brother. Don't think you need me for basic finance, bro."

"And yet," Pete said, his hand still tight on his brother's arm, "you look thin. You could use a steak."

"What about your visit with the babies?" Jack asked.

Pete looked with longing at the children. "Say goodbye to Uncle Jack, kids," Pete said. "You probably won't be seeing him for a while. I'll be back for a double visit tomorrow, and I'll bring your grandfather."

"You're a mess," Jack said, freeing his arm from his brother's grip. "It's like watching Paul Bunyan felled by one of his own trees, only those tiny seeds haven't even turned into saplings yet. In other words, they're more like termites, which is a foundational issue for you, I hope you know."

"Ha," Pete said, "keep walking and talking about Priscilla to earn your feedbag, bro. I'm all ears."

CRICKET HAD ASKED Priscilla if she was growing her business and putting down ever deeper roots in Fort Wylie in order to avoid her attraction to Pete Morgan. Priscilla had never answered her friend's question.

Pete would control her. His personality was larger than hers. Even if he didn't try to, he would, not the least because she knew her feelings for him would dictate her actions.

As a single twenty-eight-year-old woman, she found herself in a particular place in life. Many of her friends had married, begun raising families. Her parents hoped she would find a wonderful man and settle down—what parents didn't want that for their daughter?

Yet something kept telling her to treasure her independence. Who knew what storms awaited on the horizon?

Pete was a storm in her life now, buffeting her windows and threatening to blow down the door to her heart. She held fast to her common sense, knowing that of all men, a Morgan was not the man for a practical woman like her.

So she'd accepted a date tonight with a man her parents had called to say they wanted her to meet. Charlie Drumwell knew a lot about finance, her parents told her. He worked for an investment firm in Dallas.

Priscilla decided her parents weren't any subtler than Josiah Morgan in the matchmaking department. Feeling a sense of foreboding, she put on a pretty red dress, high heels, coaxed her hair into a sleek ponytail and answered the door with a smile on her face when Charlie rang the bell.

Instantly, Priscilla knew from Charlie's smiling, confident face what her parents saw in him. He was good-looking in a way that made women look twice. Clean-shaven, well-groomed to a fault, he looked like a Wall Street financier.

Nerves hit Priscilla, but she covered her anxiety with a smile. "Hello. You must be Charlie."

Of course he gave her a beautiful bouquet of flowers, his grin sure. "Yes, I'm Charlie."

"Thank you. They're lovely," she said, not wanting the flowers in her house. They'd remind her of tonight, which she already regretted. "Won't you come in?"

He stepped through the doorway, glancing around. "Quaint."

She detected slight condescension. "I like it."

"Your parents tell me you own a tea shop."

"It's in a different part of the house," Priscilla said.

To which Charlie replied, "Excellent for tax deductions."

"Yes." She put the flowers in water, then got her purse. "Did you say you had reservations for seven?"

He nodded. "You're going to love this place. It's one of my favorite restaurants."

They drove into Dallas, his silver Mercedes convertible making the drive in good time, though the minutes seemed to crawl by for Priscilla. She was used to trucks or Cricket's Volkswagen; Charlie's car seemed unnecessarily intimate. "I hope my parents didn't press you into taking me out."

He grinned. "I wanted to."

"You did?"

"Sure. I saw your picture in their living room."

They had one of her graduating from high school on their piano. "It's a very old picture."

"You look the same, don't worry."

She blushed, realizing he'd thought she was fishing for compliments. "Where are you from, Charlie?"

"Dallas. But I have an office in New York. I like it there. I like the faster pace. Still, it's great to get back to Dallas every once in a while."

He wasn't in the state much, therefore no chance for a redo of this tense date. "How did you meet my folks?"

"They came to our firm for some investment advice." He glanced at her. "Didn't they tell you?"

She shook her head.

"Oh. Then I suppose I shouldn't have mentioned it. Please excuse my slip. Very unprofessional."

She wondered why her folks hadn't said anything. Usually they discussed everything with her. "I haven't been by to see them much lately, unfortunately."

"Well, it will all work out." He turned on some soothing classical music, and Priscilla frowned.

"What will all work out?"

Charlie cleared his throat. "I meant that you'll see them soon, I'm sure."

An undercurrent of tension colored his otherwise offhand comment. Priscilla felt certain this was no casual night out. Her parents had been with the same bank in Fort Wylie for years—why would they be moving their money now? Not knowing what to say, Priscilla looked out the window and wondered what Pete was doing tonight.

IN A SMALL CAFÉ in Union Junction, Pete studied his brother Jack carefully as they wolfed down burgers and tea at a local hamburger joint. He'd forgotten Jack didn't drink alcohol. He couldn't recall why, either, but maybe he just wanted to be as different from Pop as possible. Pete decided Jack looked lean but not hungry; for a thirty-two-year-old, he lived a fairly clean life he called his own. "You've been hanging around these parts a lot lately," Pete observed. "It's been good to see you."

Jack shrugged. "I like the Lonely Hearts Station rodeo."

"Got a lady friend?"

Jack eyed him over a french fry. "Must you ask?"

"You asked me about Priscilla," Pete reminded him without rancor. Jack had always been private, though they'd been close as kids.

"True," Jack said, "but that doesn't mean I want to talk about women. I merely wanted to warn you that your friend is in financial straits."

Pete frowned. "She hasn't mentioned it."

"Who would? I wouldn't."

"So why would you care enough about her to mention it to me?"

"I like her. I like Cricket." Jack grinned. "Pop's

batting a thousand, the jackass. Lucky for me, I'm not part of his game. And his letter signed me off from any responsibility."

"Yeah. That's great. Leave it to the rest of us to patch things up with the old man." Pete was starving. He couldn't remember the last time he'd eaten a full meal, and then realized why—he hadn't been cooking. "Jeez, I don't think Pop's eaten anything decent in days."

"What the hell?" Jack asked. "Do you have to feed him like a baby?"

"I look out for him since we're under the same roof." Pete wondered how much he could say about Pop without Jack heading out like a streak of spring lightning. "He can't really get to a restaurant himself. Tires him out."

Jack sighed. "Can we have a Pop-free discussion? I'm only here to talk about Priscilla and what you're going to do about her. Although I don't mind if you babble about those babies, even if you're crazy to want all of them." Jack chewed on his burger with the contentment of a single bachelor. "Can't you start small? Like with just one?"

"No," Pete stated flatly. "And I don't plan to do anything about Priscilla, unless there's something you recommend?"

Jack shook his head. "I do no recommending. Unlike the root of our family tree, I mind my own business."

"Good policy." Pete was bothered, more than he wanted to admit, about Priscilla. "So when you say that nothing this rodeo-finance friend of yours told you isn't common knowledge, to what exactly are you referring? Priscilla has never mentioned that her parents are having issues. I knew about her tea shop having some financial difficulties—Pop tried to bribe her to marry me—but she seems to be too independent to fall for Pop's game."

"Yeah, well," Jack said, "I hate to be the bearer of bad news, but since it'll be in the newspaper next week, the Perkinses have a small bankruptcy problem."

Pete's brows shot up. "Bankruptcy is not small."

"No." Jack leaned back in the booth. "In fact, it's large. Apparently their money was invested with someone who helped them lose a vast portion of it."

"Holy smokes." Pete blinked. "There's no way any bank will accept a co-sign from a bankrupt party."

"No." His brother sighed. "I figure Priscilla stands to lose her home and her tea shop."

"I don't understand how this could happen." Pete thought about his father's worldwide holdings and wondered why one country-living man could be so financially wise, while others who had the best financial help available found themselves in deep swamp water. "Just like that, everything is gone?"

Jack nodded. "Don't know what they were invested in. A lot of stocks is what I heard, though I don't know that for sure. It's not as if they were spending money like water or anything. They just had bad financial advice and had trusted their broker. These are tricky times we live in."

"I'm amazed at your ability to know things about people. I have basically three tracks on my mind, and anything that's not currently revolving on one of those three tracks gets sifted out quickly."

"Kids'll do that to you," Jack said with a grin. "It's called baby blues or something."

Pete shook his head. "No, it's not. That's what the woman gets."

"No," Jack said, "I'm pretty sure you've got them." He tossed his napkin to the table. "I'll buy this round."

Pete shook his head, trying to snatch the dinner check Jack had taken from the curvy waitress. "I owe you something for the information."

"Thought you said Priscilla doesn't mean anything to you."

Pete threw his brother a wry look. "I'm always interested in people I know."

"Still, I'll pay." Jack grinned. "You may wind up paying for a wife and four kids. You're going to be eating meat loaf for the rest of your life unless you have a major nest egg tucked away."

"You and I should go into business together," Pete said, making Jack's eyebrows hover under his cowboy hat.

"Family ventures are risky," Jack said, jumping up from the table. *"Bon appetit."*

He kissed the waitress on the cheek on his way out of the restaurant, disappearing just like Pete had known he would. Yet his brother had left behind some serious information. Pete's gut roiled and it wasn't because the burger had been bad. Priscilla would be devastated if she lost her business—that was putting it mildly. He had to think she would also be crushed to learn of her parents' financial misfortune.

Maybe Jack was wrong. He lived in another town, after all. He barely knew Priscilla.

Pete's chest tightened. He had a bad feeling Jack wouldn't have driven all the way to Union Junction if the story wasn't fact. Jack had a mind like Pop's, with an incredible nose for detail. Pete didn't notice the waitress refill his tea glass. He drummed his fingers on the table, lost in the maze of what he'd learned and what it might mean to those he cared about.

Chapter Ten

That night, Pete arrived home later than usual. He found Josiah waiting up for him, his face drawn as he reclined in his chair. "Hey, Pop," Pete said. "How are you doing?"

"Could be better," Josiah said. Pete figured that was likely true, especially if Pop knew that his first-born son had been in town and couldn't be dragged home for a short hello.

"Where have you been?" Josiah demanded.

"I grabbed a burger. I should have called and asked you if you wanted me to bring you one. Sorry about that." He'd grabbed a beer from the fridge and now sat down in the darkened den with his father.

"You'll never believe who paid me a surprise visit," Josiah said.

"I probably won't." Pete's heart jumped. Maybe Priscilla had stopped by. She liked visiting Pop.

"A social worker from the county." Josiah's white brows beetled as he glanced at Pete.

Pete's heart began a serious hammering. "Social worker?"

Josiah nodded. "Yep. To sort of check us out. The informal beginning of what she called a 'home study.'" He sighed. "Wish you'd been here. Don't think I made a great impression."

Pete shook his head. "I thought they typically made appointments for that sort of thing."

"I guess not if they're trying to find out how we really live, so we can't stage ourselves just to look good for the caseworkers. At least that's the way I figured it."

"Wow." Pete's chest tightened. "I wish I'd been here, too. Don't they have to meet me as the prospective father?"

"As I say, I suspect this was very informal, just a look-see, maybe to make certain we weren't weirdoes or completely unsuitable. For all they know, I suppose we could be…I don't know, totally odd." Josiah looked sheepish. "Anyway, I think we have a bit of a reputation in Union Junction."

"We? I haven't been here long enough to have a reputation." Pete tensed, sensing danger. This was so important to him—the fate of four little babies hung in the balance—and he could tell Pop was prevaricating, loath to share everything that had transpired.

"Apparently my parenting skills have been the topic of some discussion in the town over the years," Josiah said. "Much rumor and nonsense, of course, because all my sons have turned out quite well, thank you. In contrast to some other folks who reared wimps," he stated. "But I digress."

"You're not the father in consideration, Pop. And you're right—they shouldn't make any judgments based on whatever gossip has circulated over the years. It's not fair."

Josiah nodded. "I'm afraid I was half dozing when the caseworker arrived—a meticulous old woman named Mrs. Corkindale. A dragon, if you ask me."

"Pop," Pete said desperately, realizing that Mrs. Corkindale and Pop hadn't exactly taken to each other, "just the facts, please."

"All right." Josiah sighed. "I was half asleep. I'd had a wee bit of my 'medicine,' as is my custom. The house wasn't dusted or vacuumed." He glanced around. "She did everything but look under my chair for dust bunnies and monsters and maybe even a dead body or two."

"Okay, Pop," Pete said. "So you were tipsy and sleepy and not yourself, and she gave the house the white-glove treatment? Is that a problem?"

"Well, I exaggerate a bit," Josiah said. "She didn't exactly whip out white gloves, but I could see her eyeballs jumping from surface to surface. Hideous old witch," Josiah grumbled. "I should have asked her where she hid her broom."

Pete rubbed his face, his heart sinking. "She should have talked to me, not you."

"Right. Well, she'll be back. At least she said she would." Josiah frowned. "You couldn't be unluckier in your assignment of social worker. In all my years, I never met such an unlikable woman."

Pete sighed. "Pop, it's all right. Don't fret." It warmed his heart to see how badly his father wanted to see the quadruplets remain together, with one family who would love them. In his eyes, the Morgans could provide that easily. "We have a lot of experience in being a big family. There aren't many like us who can take on and afford the care of an entire family. Let's just keep our fingers crossed and pray."

"And rub our rabbit's feet and throw salt over our shoulders and eat four-leaf clovers for breakfast," Josiah said, grumpier than Pete had seen him recently. "I wish I hadn't answered the door."

"Pop," Pete murmured, shocked that his father would dismiss the power of prayer and hope. *He'd be even more despondent if he knew Jack had been within a stone's throw of the ranch.* Pete felt a heaviness in his soul. Jack had issues. Priscilla's business was in trouble, her family in bigger trouble, if Jack was correct. Pop was ill, and the babies were no closer to being in the home where Pete felt certain they belonged.

Something had to give soon. Being a Morgan was starting to feel like a curse.

THE NEXT DAY Pete didn't wait for Mrs. Corkindale to pop in again. He went straight to her office, demanding to see her—in the most accommodating, least-scary voice he could manage. He was determined that, no matter the gossip, she would see him as a softie and, unlike Pop, responsible and vigilant against the formation of dust bunnies and other elements of untidy living.

"Hello," Mrs. Corkindale said, coming out from her office. "How can I help you?"

"I understand you stopped by the Morgan ranch yesterday," Pete said. "My father said I missed you. I'm Pete Morgan."

She looked him over briefly. "Yes. Mr. Morgan and I had an entertaining visit."

He raised his brows, not certain if that was good or bad. Pop could definitely be amusing, but depending on the entertainment, anything might have happened. "I was wondering if there are any questions you wanted to ask me."

She shook her head. "Not at this time. Yesterday's visit was an informal inspection of the premises. I understand you haven't lived there long."

"I haven't, actually. I've been on active duty." He didn't offer further details.

"And your father hasn't been there long."

"He just returned from France, actually. He had some real estate holdings over there he was managing."

She smiled thinly. "Has he been ill?"

Pete realized that although Mrs. Corkindale claimed she had no questions to ask him, he was getting a sample of what he assumed must be a twenty-page questionnaire. Now was not the time to step in a minefield. His mind went into sharp focus, the way it did when he was on assignment. "Pop has been facing some health issues. He keeps busy, though."

She looked at him. "I imagine it's difficult to take care of an aging parent. Many households in the country find themselves with the added burden of elderly care. It's not easy."

He saw where she was going with that. "No one takes care of Pop. He's far too independent for that."

"Yet there may come a day when you might have to assume more of his care. Have you considered that as you think about becoming a father to several children?"

Pete shrugged. "I have two married brothers who live close by. We all keep an eye on Pop. But as I say, he won't put up with much coddling. Did he tell you he's been halter-breaking a new horse recently?"

She shook her head.

"He's pretty determined to keep his mind on matters besides his health," Pete said mildly. "Pop's always been a fighter."

"We have to be practical, Mr. Morgan. I'm sure you appreciate that. Our first concern has to be the children."

"That's good," he said. "Then I'm sure you recognize the amount of resources we have at hand to deal with adopting four children. We have lots of family, a large home and the desire to make them a special part of our lives."

She looked at him a long time. "Thank you for stopping by, Mr. Morgan. I've got some meetings I must attend. Please tell your father I said hello. And that I hope his gout is better."

Pete blinked. "I will." *Gout?*

She stepped back inside her office, the impromptu interview over. Pete's heart sank. Like Pop, he wasn't sure what to think of Mrs. Corkindale. Did they have even a snowball's chance in hell?

Feeling as though he'd missed his mission, Pete departed, jumping into his truck. He'd never felt so dejected.

His spirit dragged. He drew a long sigh, then decided he might as well not put off his second errand of the day.

Certainly matters couldn't get worse.

PRISCILLA SAT in her tea shop, the Closed sign adorning the window. It was past five o'clock, and the sun was fading in the winter sky. She had a lot of cleaning to do, but for ten minutes, as soon as she'd locked the door, she'd been sitting here, thinking. Frozen.

Her worried parents had paid her a surprise visit today, telling her in a tear-filled conversation that next week's newspaper would list them as having filed for bankruptcy.

In black-and-white, everything she'd thought was secure would be exposed as fragile. But the worst part had been seeing the shock and concern on her parents' sweet faces. They'd always made sure she'd had whatever she needed, and now she felt so helpless, being unable to return some of their reassurance, support and assistance.

She would also lose her tea shop. If she closed the business for good, she could probably hang on to her house if she went back to work at her previous job. Tears threatened, but she refused to cry about her situation. Small businesses were notoriously hard to keep afloat—she'd known the odds would be challenging when she opened the shop. She'd had more than her fair share of good luck and support from the community. There was no shame in admitting that her first attempt at a business didn't make it. Later on, she could start over, make a run at it again with the experience and knowledge she'd gained.

She'd have to tell Cricket, which would be heart-breaking. Yet there was no reason to tie her good friend to her financial dilemma. By next week everyone would know that the once-wealthy Perkins family had suffered a great loss.

She felt sorry for her parents. They hadn't complained, but she knew that they'd believed their golden years were financially secure.

A knock sounded on the tea-room door, and for the first time since she'd owned the shop, she asked herself why people never seemed to understand the meaning of Closed.

She acknowledged this was a crabby thing to

think. Many times someone had caught her just as she was locking up, usually a mom racing from work to grab cookies for a surprise for her children, and Priscilla had always felt very blessed for the customers who considered her shop a good choice for their needs.

She could see a cowboy hat through the glass, and what appeared to be Pete's face. Priscilla went to open the door.

"I know you're closed," Pete said, "but I have to talk to you."

"I'm glad you're here," Priscilla said. "You'll be good company."

"I will?" Pete asked.

"Well, I think so," Priscilla said. "You're amusing. Maybe not as fun as your father is, but you're interesting."

"I don't know that anyone has ever called Pop fun."

She smiled. "Do you want a cookie and some tea?"

"If I'm buying, I'll buy for both of us."

"Today I'll let you. I still need to clean up, but if you don't mind waiting—"

"Hey, I'll help." Pete took off his shearling jacket, laid it over a chair and began picking up coffee cups, tea glasses and dessert plates. "Glad I caught you. I should have called first, but I was really of two minds about coming. Debated with myself all the way over here, and then decided I'd let the chips fall where they may."

She watched him as he carried things into the small kitchen, a big, broad-shouldered man carrying tiny pieces of china, and felt a strange shift in her heart. What was it about him that drew her, compared to the complete lack of feeling she experienced during her date with a clean-cut, financially driven man like Charlie? That evening had been just short of a disaster, though he'd sent her flowers and left a message on her voice mail saying how much he'd like to see her again. Her skin crawled just a bit at the thought of enduring another date with Charlie. "Pete, you don't have to do that. You sit while I clean. Just having the company is enough."

"Nah," he said. "In my house, everyone pitches in with the chores."

"You can't pay *and* work," she said. "If you work in the kitchen, you get a free snack."

He nodded. "All right. Where's the broom? I think my little nieces and nephew must have been eating in this chair."

Priscilla laughed. "They weren't here, but I did have several moms who were here with their kids. It was fun." She handed him the broom and dustpan and began clearing the other tables. "So tell me what this big emergency is all about. Your father is fine, I'm sure."

"Pop's a bull," Pete said. "A social worker paid a call to the ranch when I wasn't there." He looked at her, and Priscilla raised her brows to show that she understood the significance of the adoption process slowly starting. "Well, Pop being Pop and tough as cowhide didn't bother to share his actual health conditions and told her he'd been resting because he had gout in his foot."

Priscilla smiled. "Clever Josiah."

"So Pop is fine. Not the most truthful person, but he's fine." Pete finished sweeping and put the broom away. "He got into such a snit over the caseworker's surprise visit—he'd been napping off the effects of a little of his afternoon self-medicating—and he's convinced she's a dragon out to cut him down in his prime. He says he's giving up drinking altogether. Not that he was that big a drinker, but he's even taken to wearing nice jeans and a dress shirt in case she sneaks up on him again."

Priscilla laughed. "I'm sorry. I know it's not funny, but there is a little humor in it." She smiled at Pete. "He really wants those children, doesn't he?"

"More than you can imagine. Well, I guess you can imagine, since he tried to hire you to be my wife to make my résumé a little more apple-shiny to the adoption folks."

The smile left her face as she went back to cleaning. "Shall we take tea and cookies into the house? I must admit I'm not much in the mood to relax in here tonight, although it used to be my favorite place for a cozy winding-down."

"That would be great. Give me something to carry."

Priscilla locked up, turned out all the lights

except for a small lamp she always left burning, and handed Pete a tray with a teapot and cookies on a plate. "There's more in the house if we decide we have an appetite."

"Mmm," Pete said. "When I was a kid, we used to sneak our grilled cheese sandwiches and milk outside to eat. We weren't supposed to—Mom was afraid we'd get our food dirty—but she couldn't be mad at us because we loved picnicking so much. This feels like a picnic."

"Did you get your food dirty? Was Mom right?" Priscilla asked, leading him through the door that adjoined her residence to the tea shop. "Little boys probably spill milk and drop food easily."

"We had a five-second rule for dropped sandwiches, but hungry boys eat pretty quick. Over time, Mom got tired of worrying about dirt and kept a picnic blanket in the kitchen pantry we could grab if we wanted it." He grinned as he followed her. "It was plastic and durable. That red-checked thing is probably still around the house somewhere."

They went to the kitchen so Priscilla could set the teapot on a warmer. Each of them took a white-painted chair at the table. Priscilla smiled at him. "So I'm dying to hear your news."

"This isn't really news," Pete said slowly, and she saw his face tense. "This is gossip. I can't reveal the source, but it bothered me enough to come ask you in person."

Her heart began beating more quickly. "Gossip about me?"

He nodded. "I want to help you, if you need help."

Her eyes went wide; her pounding heart seemed to hesitate. Surely he didn't know already about her family's financial problems. She needed a few days to process the information, knowing it would soon be in the paper for everyone to see. She needed to get the face she'd present to the world ready. "I'm fine, Pete. Whatever you've heard, I assure you I'm fine." She *was* going to be fine, no matter what.

He took a deep breath. "I really don't know a good way to say this. Please forgive me if I'm not as smooth as I could be. I've been a loner for so long that I'm not good at casual chatter. But a reliable source says your parents are—"

She jumped to her feet. She couldn't help herself— it was a reflex she had no control over. "My parents are just fine," she told him emphatically.

He looked at her, and his deep blue eyes held concern and sympathy, the same eyes she'd once thought glacial and hard. He didn't say another word. He probably didn't have to, given her abrupt denial.

Priscilla sat back down with a humiliated sigh. "Talk about an overreaction…"

Pete smiled. "I have lots of those, too."

"No, you don't. You're always cool and in control."

"Is that what you see? It's not the way my stomach feels." He winked at her. "On the other hand, I'm tough. Strong. Manly."

He pulled the smile from her he wanted. "Okay, tough guy. Go on with the story."

His hesitation was prolonged, and she couldn't blame him for not wanting to bring up the topic again. "There was some talk that your parents are in a tight spot."

"They are." It was probably best to just admit what he already knew and adopt the brave face he wore. He was right—the butterflies in her tummy remained despite the facade, but she preferred the direct approach rather than being the scared bunny she felt like.

"I'm sorry."

"It's all right," she said quickly. "The Perkinses are tough. We'll recreate ourselves. It will be a bit harder this time, maybe, but my family is resilient."

"Good girl." His gaze held admiration. "Is there anything I can do to help? I know a little something about needing to recreate one's self, tough times, brave faces and all that."

"You can tell me who told you," she said. "It's not supposed to be in the paper until next week."

"It's not common knowledge," he assured her. "Don't worry. You still have a little time to digest."

"Ah. Josiah working the grapevine again?"

"It was one of my brothers." Pete shrugged. "And

not the brother I've considered well-informed. He's taking on some of Pop's characteristics."

"Jack," she said, and he nodded.

"He'll keep it quiet," Pete told her. "He only told me because he knows that you and I are…friends."

Her gaze jumped to his. The word *friends* lingered in the air between them. It felt as if they were something more than that, Priscilla admitted to herself.

"Will you be all right?" Pete asked softly.

"I'll be closing the tea shop," she said, and suddenly, the tears she'd been hiding behind her brave face pricked her eyes, making her nose a little runny. "I'm so sorry. It's just now starting to hit me."

"Uh-oh," Pete said, and put out his arms to envelop her. She went into them without hesitation, sitting on his lap, allowing herself to accept the comfort of his broad, warm chest, his strong shoulders. Once she was in his embrace, she realized how good he smelled, how right he felt, and closing her eyes, she let herself cry for a moment.

Pete stroked Priscilla's hair silently. He felt terrible for her. His purpose in coming here tonight had been to find out if there was anything he could do to help, specifically financially. He'd fully intended to offer her assistance with the tea shop, knowing how much work and heart she'd put into it. As his father had noted, however, Priscilla didn't have a price, and now that his worst fears were confirmed, he didn't dare offer money. She wanted bolstering, she wanted a friendly ear. So he sat holding her, trying to be the friend she seemed to need right now. "I am so sorry," he finally said, his voice thick.

"I am, too. But I'm not the first person who's found themselves with reduced fortunes. The downturn in the economy has been hard on a lot of people." She pulled away, blew her nose on a tissue and laughed, clearly embarrassed by her tears. "I feel silly for weeping on you. There are more important things in life than a tea shop."

"It's your livelihood," Pete said quietly. "You're entitled to be disappointed."

She nodded. "Thanks. But I've kept in touch with my old boss over the past two years, so I know I can go back to work at my job. Later on, when things settle down, I can start over."

He nodded, releasing her gently. "That's the spirit."

She returned to her chair. "So, did you drive all the way out here just to find out if what you'd heard was true?"

"Yes, and I wanted to know if there was anything I could do to help." He shrugged. "I'm good at packing."

She smiled. "You're a hero. But I'll manage. You've got a father who needs you, and maybe, if you can win over your father's nemesis, four new children. I think you'll have your hands full."

"Never too full for a friend, though." He grinned at her. "You know I'll be looking for a nanny if I get the children."

"Oh." She wiped her nose, smiled a bit soggily. "I thought you were going to say you could use a companion for your father."

"I need to do something for Pop, but I haven't quite determined what it is." Pete looked at her. "Will you really close the shop?"

She nodded. "It's for the best. I don't want a bankruptcy on my credit. I have no way to pay back my bank loan, now that it's increased. I'd asked Cricket to be my partner, but I refuse to drag her into this."

He sat thinking for a minute, wishing there was some way he could help her. But there was nothing he could do, not for the circumstances she found herself in. The pity of it was she was very talented at running a business people enjoyed. She was frugal; she had a good product.

He shook his head. "I'll help you in any way I can. You know that."

"Thanks." Priscilla reached over and briefly put her hand over his. He reveled in her touch. The worst part about being friends, he realized, was that there were specific lines he couldn't cross.

Such as he couldn't tell her how much he cared about her, how much it pained him to see her hurting. He wanted to sweep her into his arms, carry her away, reassure her.

Instead, he said gruffly, half-teasing, speaking his mind out loud, but doing his best to sound casual, "Don't forget I'm always looking for a bride."

She looked at him, her expression wry. "I just happen to be in the market for a husband."

Chapter Eleven

"Are you?" Pete asked, hardly daring to hope that Priscilla was telling him that she'd marry him. He'd marry her in a heartbeat.

"Of course I'm in the market for a husband," Priscilla said. "All my friends are married, except Cricket. I'd like to settle down one day."

"Hey," he said, puffing out his chest, "there's always me, the guy from Union Junction."

She smiled at him. "You'd be my first choice."

"Now we're getting somewhere," Pete said, "because you'd be mine, too. And I think we know where my father stands on the issue."

She shook her head. "What about all the women at the matchmaking party?"

"Oh, nice women, all of them. But there was a reason Pop picked you first."

"Maybe he'd heard I had a crush on you," Priscilla said. "You know how the grapevine operates in small towns."

"I doubt it. You play your cards tighter to your chest than a man."

"I thought you were going to say 'than a spy,'" she teased.

"Yeah, well, a spy, too." Pete shook his head. "At least that's James Bond's trademark."

"Were you that kind of spy?" she asked gently.

He looked at her. "Who told you?"

"A little birdie." She shrugged. "My lips are sealed."

He looked at those soft, sweet lips and wished they were sealed to all but him. He was dying to kiss her.

"I sort of figure I served my country, now I'm going to serve four babies if I get the chance." He reached over and took her hand in his, tapping her fingers with his. The gesture was playful, and yet he was holding her just the same. "I need a partner in crime."

"I told you why I can't," she murmured.

"Think of it as redemption."

She sucked in a startled breath. "Redemption?"

"Sure. We all deserve a second chance."

Her gaze held his while she contemplated his words.

"If you think about it, you'd be doing me a helluva favor," Pete said. "I've been lonely for a long time."

"Who's getting rescued here?" she asked, slipping her hand from his.

"Both of us could use a life preserver, me more than you."

And then he took her hand back in his, raising it to his lips, and gently kissed her fingers. Priscilla closed her eyes, and then to his utter shock, she said, "Let's go to bed and sleep on it."

He blinked, wondering if he'd just received the invitation of all invitations. She rose from her chair, turned off the tea warmer and dimmed the kitchen lights. "Let me show you the rest of the house," she said.

He followed quickly, not about to miss the grand tour. His Adam's apple felt permanently lodged north of where it belonged. He noticed she skipped the parlor, the main family room and whatever else was on the first floor as she led him up the staircase. The wood creaked a bit under his weight. He tried to walk softly, feeling as if he was being taken to a reverent place. Priscilla drew him into her bedroom, and he had a quick glance at white-lace curtains and a floral comforter before she took his hat and put it on a chair. She turned the lights low, and the next thing Pete knew, he had an armful of warm, inviting woman.

This is heaven. Please let me get through the pearly gates.

PRISCILLA HAD KNOWN that being with Pete would be a wonderful experience. What she hadn't imagined was that he would be so kind, so gentle, so loving. He was an amazing lover, everything she might ever have hoped for.

Now her heart was fully engaged. She stroked one palm down his chest as he slept; seeing that he hadn't moved, she swept her hand lightly over the hard ridges of his abdomen. He was just as beautiful asleep as he was awake, his dark beauty against the white of her sheets giving her eyes plenty to admire.

Suddenly his hand caught hers, arresting it as it stroked his skin. Her gaze flew to his. He gave her a sleepy, caught-ya smile—and then he rolled over, kissing her as he made certain her curiosity was completely satisfied.

THE NEXT MORNING Pete heard his cell phone ringing in his jeans pocket, the jeans he'd left carelessly on the floor last night as he had found his fortunate way into Priscilla's bed. She was still asleep, a vision of relaxed, happy beauty if ever he'd seen it. He quickly reached for the phone so it wouldn't awaken her. "Hello?"

"Son, where are you?" his father demanded.

"I'm, um—"

"Never mind," Pop said. "That social worker's coming by in three hours. Guess she felt like she could make an appointment this time, instead of doing a drop-in."

"What's going on?" Pete asked, getting up, grabbing for his jeans.

"I don't know. But I think this time you ought to be here. We don't want it to look like you're never around."

"True." He cast a glance at Priscilla. She was now fully awake, watching him, the sheet pulled close to her chin. He grinned at her modesty. It would do her no good. The next time he lay in a bed with her, he was going to make certain there was nothing around for her to be modest with. She had the sexiest, most made-for-him body—he wasn't about to let her hide it from him. "Okay, Pop, I'll get there as fast as I can."

"Bring Priscilla," his father said. "Always helps to have a female around." He hung up, sounding rushed.

Pete tucked the cell phone back into the jeans he was sliding over his butt. "Sorry about that."

"Is everything all right?" Priscilla asked.

He leaned to kiss her, taking his time about it. "Unfortunately I'm going to have to be less than a gentleman and head home, though I'd prefer to stay and offer you breakfast."

"That's not necessary," Priscilla said.

Still, he hated to leave her. "If you go to Union Junction with me, I can definitely offer you breakfast."

She looked at him. "Just breakfast?"

He smiled. "Is there something else you want?"

He liked the blush that warmed her cheeks. "I meant, is there anything going on I should know about? Your father doesn't often call you home at eight o'clock in the morning, does he?"

Pete shook his head. "The social worker is stopping by. Pop's nervous."

She got up, grabbed some clothes. "I don't know. Sounds like you have a lot on your hands."

"Pop says you'd probably be good to have around."

She stopped, looked at him. "Why?"

He shrugged. "You know Pop. He has his reasons for everything, and they're usually convoluted."

"I see," she said, gazing at him with clear, wide eyes.

"I think he believes you can present the softer side of the Morgan men," he admitted, unable to fib to those trusting eyes.

She looked at him for a long time, and then much to his surprise, she said, "Give me fifteen minutes for a quick shower, and I'll ride out there with you."

"What about the tea shop?" He was surprised by her quick agreement to accompany him.

She took a long, deep breath to steady herself. She said, "Truthfully, I need to escape for a few days."

He realized she was thinking about her parents' situation and how soon it would become public knowledge. He nodded. "I've got a great place to escape to."

"There comes a time in every woman's life when she looks for redemption," she said.

Pete thought, *Men, too,* though he didn't say it out loud. There was no reason to scare her off. That was the last thing he wanted to do.

"You can be my stand-in fiancée," he said, half teasing, thinking how much that would suit him. Would she ever agree to being a for-real fiancée? "Make me look good to the social worker and all the other cogs and wheels deciding my fate."

"Isn't it bad to lie?"

"It's terrible to lie." He kissed her sweet lips, taking his time. "You could always make it true."

She stepped away, looking at him with surprise. Her eyes searched his, but if she thought he was teasing, she wasn't going to find laughter lurking in his expression. He was deadly serious—anything to do with the babies brought out his most sober side.

"I'm going to shower," she said, "and be ready as fast as I can."

She ignored his proposal. He figured he would, too, if he were her. As proposals went, it was spur-of-the-moment, pathetic, not very romantic. Still, he felt he'd made major headway by talking her into going with him to Union Junction, knowing that the babies were the mission.

Yet it looked strangely like a surrender when Priscilla turned off the lights in the house and put a Closed Until Further Notice sign in her tea-shop window.

WHEN PETE AND Priscilla arrived at the ranch, they couldn't find Josiah anywhere. Pete couldn't raise him on his cell phone, and he wasn't in the barns. "It's not like him to be far from the action," Pete murmured. Pop was a big man and he knew how to take care of himself. There was no reason to worry; he'd show up soon enough. His truck was there, so he hadn't run for groceries. He wasn't tidying up the house, which certainly needed a dusting, Pete thought, deciding to tackle it himself. Priscilla helped him, and they quickly made the den area presentable.

"I thought he'd be back by now," Pete said.

Priscilla shook her head. "I'm still trying to figure out my own parents. I don't dare try to figure out Josiah."

Pete's anxiety notched up a bit. He wanted his father around for the caseworker's visit, even though it wasn't Pop applying to become the father of the quadruplets. He could use all the moral support he could get.

The doorbell rang, and Pete drew a deep breath. "Here goes," he said to Priscilla, glad for her quiet companionship, and opened the door.

The caseworker looked at him. "Hello, Mr. Morgan."

"Hello, Mrs. Corkindale. Nice to see you again."

She stepped past him as he indicated, stopping when she saw Priscilla. "Hello."

"Hi. I'm Priscilla Perkins," Priscilla said, extending her hand.

The social worker considered her. "Perkins?"

"Yes, ma'am."

"My fiancée," Pete added. Priscilla glanced at him, startled. They hadn't confirmed their plan, but he knew she wouldn't mind the ruse.

He hoped Mrs. Corkindale would be impressed by Priscilla's warmth as much as he was. It seemed like the moment to grab good fortune and run with it. Priscilla had just agreed to help him by being a pretend fiancée, hadn't she? That wasn't terribly dishonest—it was all for the babies, wasn't it? Although maybe one day he could convince her to be his true fiancée. He suddenly realized how much he really wanted that. Making love to her had changed him forever; deep in his heart, where commitment and denial had once warred, lay nothing but contentment.

Mrs. Corkindale smiled at Priscilla. "I knew some Perkinses once."

Priscilla smiled. "Did you?"

"Yes." She nodded her head, thinking.

And then it hit him. Mrs. Corkindale would have handled hundreds of adoption cases over the years. Priscilla glanced at him, her eyes wide, though she kept the friendly smile on her face. He shrugged as if to say, "No big deal."

"Do you remember where you knew some Perkinses, Mrs. Corkindale?" Priscilla asked. "My parents have no relatives around here. We live in Fort Wylie."

Mrs. Corkindale seemed perplexed. "Perhaps I've gotten the names confused."

Priscilla smiled. "I do that all the time."

Pete grinned, glad the moment was over. "Well, I—"

Mrs. Corkindale snapped her fingers. "I think there was someone named Perkins in the newspaper today."

"The newspaper?" Priscilla went very still, her smile slipping. "How could that be?"

Priscilla's parents had said the bankruptcy wouldn't be listed for a few days. Pete went to snatch the paper off of Pop's recliner, where it always was.

On the front page were the top bankruptcies of note in the state. The Perkinses were listed fifth, with the greatest amount of personal fortune lost. Silently he handed the paper to Priscilla.

"Oh, my," Mrs. Corkindale said. "I am so sorry."

But Priscilla didn't hear that. She was lost, staring at the newspaper, this black-and-white harbinger of doom.

Chapter Twelve

Priscilla couldn't shake the fog of panic suddenly enveloping her. She stared at her family's names in the newspaper, completely stunned. She'd known it was coming; it didn't make it any easier to take.

It was humiliating, but she knew her parents must be heartbroken and ashamed.

She glanced up, finding Pete's sympathetic gaze on her. Mrs. Corkindale cleared her throat uncomfortably. "Perhaps I've come at a bad time," she said.

Priscilla blinked. This was Pete's big moment to try to convince the state that he was a fit father for the babies, and the spotlight was on her. "Pete, I think I'm going to go sit in the kitchen and call my folks while you and Mrs. Corkindale talk."

"All right," Pete said, obviously worried about her. But she didn't want him to be concerned; she would be fine. She wanted to get away from his watchful gaze.

"If you'll excuse me, Mrs. Corkindale," she

murmured, and slipped away. She heard Pete and the social worker move into another room, and though she knew it would be good manners to take Mrs. Corkindale a glass of iced tea, she instead slipped out the front door to catch a breath of icy air.

"What's happening in there?" Josiah demanded from his place on the front porch. He sat in a rocker, wrapped in a blanket, his craggy face worn with concern.

She looked at him. "Why are you skulking out here?"

"I'm not skulking. I'm eavesdropping."

"How can you eavesdrop? You're not even near the door." Priscilla sat down on the step close to where his rocking chair was. "I don't remember that chair being on the porch."

"I moved it up here so I could look at the view."

"Just now?"

"Yes. Is there a reason my rocker is of such interest to you, young lady?"

"Not at all." She turned to look at the view he suddenly found so interesting. "Just wondered when you became a rocking-chair enthusiast. I always saw you more as an action kind of man."

He sniffed. "I've still got plenty of pepper left in me, don't you worry. How's it going in there?"

"Don't you know, since you're eavesdropping?"

He tried to look innocent. "Apparently I'm not the best spy this family has."

She sighed. "Pete's big moment could have started off better without me as a conversation item."

"Meaning?"

"Mrs. Corkindale had read today's paper, of course. Probably with her morning coffee, after she milked twenty cows. Energetic lady, Mrs. Corkindale."

"Ah," Josiah said, "you're upset."

She blew out a breath. "I am. And though I shouldn't have made that persnickety comment, I'll admit to being highly embarrassed."

He gazed at her. "You shouldn't be embarrassed. Your folks are good people."

"I know. But Pete had introduced me as his fiancée, and—"

"Aha!" Josiah exclaimed. "I knew you two would hit it off! After a few sparks, of course, perhaps even a forest fire or two, but I've never seen two people more perfect for each other." He beamed, delighted. "This is great news! Congratulations."

"Josiah," Priscilla said, eager to make him understand, "it was just a front to help Pete for the adoption application. For the sake of the babies. He asked me to help him look more…"

"Stable," Josiah said, his grin huge. "More like a family man."

"Something like that," she admitted, not pleased that he was still so thrilled.

He looked up at the sky, appearing to thank the heavens. She, however, didn't feel quite so thankful.

Had she not made love with Pete, if she could call back those wonderful moments they'd shared together, perhaps she wouldn't feel so guilty knowing that she may have adversely affected his chances with the adoption. It certainly couldn't look good that his "fiancée" had parents who were in financial distress. And she was in the same boat, a fact that probably wouldn't be too difficult for the caseworker to learn. Financial distress, particularly a bankruptcy, sometimes spelled "irresponsible" to outside eyes. And worse, it could sometimes even appear that possible shady dealings had gone on.

She shouldn't have allowed herself to fall into Pete's arms, shouldn't have come out here today to escape her problems. The worst part was that no matter how much she rationalized all this, making love with Pete had been the most magical time of her life.

"Pete and I are not as alike as you think," she told Josiah, a bit more sternly than she'd intended. "We're very different."

Josiah nodded. "Like cinnamon and sugar. Meat and potatoes. It's good to be different." He smiled again. "We'll go out to lunch after Mrs. Corkindale leaves, to celebrate."

"It's just for show!" Priscilla exclaimed, exasperated. "There is no real engagement."

He shrugged. "Sometimes when a person tries on something for size, they buy. You might decide you like my son."

She did like his son. That was the problem. Priscilla eyed Josiah, noticing he'd perked up considerably. "Why were you really sitting out here?"

"Taking the fresh air, my dear. It's good for the old lungs."

"Josiah," she said, "aren't you worried that my family's problem will affect the adoption if they think Pete and I are to be married?" She shook her head. "The last thing I want is to get in the way of what Pete so dearly wants."

He looked at her, his gaze soft, and reached out to pat her hand. "It does this old heart good to know that you love my son so much, Priscilla Perkins. You'll be a fine addition to the family."

Priscilla broke her gaze from his happy one and stared off into the distance. Loving Pete wouldn't do her any good. She had her own reasons for not being more than just a temporary fiancée. It wasn't enough to love someone when you had a secret lurking in your past that affected you every day.

PETE CAME OUT onto the porch with Mrs. Corkindale thirty minutes later. Priscilla couldn't tell from Pete's face whether the conversation had gone well or not.

"Thank you for stopping by," Josiah said, rising gallantly, but Mrs. Corkindale pressed him gently back into the chair.

"Please don't get up. It is always a pleasure to be out here," she said. "The scenery is breathtaking."

Priscilla blinked. The social worker sounded friendly enough. Hopefully that meant something positive. She couldn't read Pete's face at all. He walked the woman to the car, even opening her door. The two of them spoke for a few more minutes, then Mrs. Corkindale drove away.

"How'd it go?" Josiah asked as Pete walked toward them.

"Better than I ever hoped." Pete grinned at Priscilla. "She offered me what is known as a fost-adopt situation."

"What the hell is that?" Josiah demanded. Priscilla sat frozen, waiting for Pete to explain. It was strange hearing him talk about the adoption as if it was becoming a real possibility. She felt a sense of panic welling up inside her. Had a family once sat and discussed adopting *her* child?

"It means," Pete said, "that basically the babies are ready to be released from the hospital. For a number of reasons, such as our lack of experience with infants, particularly high-needs infants, they wouldn't normally consider us. However, since we live in the county, are willing to adopt all of them and have the resources to get help for what we can't handle, should there be anything, the state is considering us. Basically a fost-adopt is that we would foster them, then they would consider whether we are a good fit for caring for the babies permanently. Adopting them."

"I raised four hellions on my own," Josiah stated. "I think I can take care of four helpless little babies."

"Pop," Pete said softly, "we don't want to underestimate the round-the-clock care these newborns will require. You need your rest, too."

Josiah glared at his son. "Don't coddle me, Pete."

Pete held up a hand, his gaze shifting to Priscilla for just a moment. "I'm just saying that I see Mrs. Corkindale's point. I'm not at all offended that they prefer an adoption with a trial basis. I'm pleased they're so concerned about the children. Frankly I didn't think I had a chance in hell of being considered." He smiled at Priscilla. "I think I owe you some thanks."

Her heart jumped. "You do?"

"You're a wonderful fiancée," he told her. "Thank you for supporting me."

She shook her head. "Mrs. Corkindale couldn't have been impressed with me. Not with my family's news in the paper." She lifted her chin. "Not that I'm apologizing for my family's circumstances."

"We wouldn't want you to, girl," Josiah said. "Would you care to take a guess at how many times I had to declare bankruptcy?"

Her eyes widened. "But you're so successful! I can't believe you ever mismanaged your affairs."

"Psh." Josiah dismissed her comment with a wave of his hand. "If I hadn't mismanaged my affairs, I might still have a wife. But that's neither here nor there. All work and no play made Josiah a dull boy—and let me tell you that working real-estate deals is no easy game. I had my share of getting eaten by the sharks. Not to mention, there are years when the economy is good and some when it stinks. I made my share of unfortunate missteps, mostly when I was younger." He put his hand to her shoulder for a moment. "Learning how to handle my finances became an all-consuming thing for me, but it shouldn't be a man's master. Your parents are more fortunate than they realize. They," he said, his voice deadly serious, "have a daughter who loves them."

Quick tears sprang into Priscilla's eyes. After a moment, Josiah got up and headed to the door.

"Congratulations," he told Pete. "I guess I don't mind baby steps, if that's the way I have to do it—and yes, I know I made a pun. Not that I'm joking about this." He clapped Pete on the back. "Good work."

He went inside. Pete stared after his father. "He doesn't look all that strong to me these days," he said to Priscilla.

"I know." Priscilla surreptitiously wiped her eyes and looked away. She was falling for Josiah as much as she had fallen for Pete. They were a special family.

He sat on the stoop next to her. "I meant what I said about you impressing Mrs. Corkindale. Her exact words were 'She seems to have a lot of confidence.'"

"Oh, not me," Priscilla said. "These days I feel less like Miss Manners and more like Miss Faking It."

She pulled slightly away from Pete's shoulder, which had naturally melded against hers as he sat down.

"About last night," he said softly, "I just want to say…I hope you have no regrets."

She did. She didn't. "Pete, I'm so scared about the adoption."

"Why? The babies will love it here. I can't wait to be a father." He turned her chin so that she faced him. "You know, you don't have to be my fiancée once they're here."

Though he meant to comfort her, arrows of reality shot into her heart. "I know," she murmured.

He removed his hand from her face. "It meant a lot that you came with me to the ranch today. Thank you."

She nodded. She didn't know what to say. She felt as if she was losing Pete by not knowing the right words, but she couldn't speak. She wanted so much to be the right woman for him, but she wasn't.

She couldn't be a mother to the children—and therefore, she couldn't be the right woman for him.

PETE KNEW EXACTLY what was bothering Priscilla. He could see she was haunted by the memory of her child, could see it in her eyes, when he talked about the babies. He understood she still mourned giving up her child. It was the same look his father wore every time he talked about his wife. Josiah would never get over losing her. He understood why she left, but he would never get over it. Pete missed his mother, too, but in all his years, Pete had never had the urge to find out where she was. She'd left them—he felt abandoned, even though he knew he was being unfair, because he didn't know the whole story.

These same demons must haunt Priscilla about her baby. Yet she'd really had no choice. She'd done as her parents had asked. She'd given away something which had torn out a piece of her heart that could never be repaired.

So he resolved to do the one thing, the only thing, that would possibly bring her peace and exorcise the past. And as a former secret agent, he knew exactly how to make that happen.

He would find out what happened to the child she'd lost, and maybe, just maybe, win her heart.

Chapter Thirteen

A week later Pete found his target. He sat outside a house an hour from Fort Wylie, waiting patiently, biding his time. Sooner or later his mission would be rewarded. His ultimate goal was that Priscilla have peace in her heart. He had the strangest feeling that she was afraid he could not love her because of her past—but he knew he had fallen in love with her from the first.

He eyed the dwelling where her son lived. The two-story, white, Cape Cod-style home was large, spacious and well kept. The street was wide, the neighborhood lined with similar homes. It looked like a comfortable place to raise a child. Quite different from the way Pete had grown up, with an absentee mother and a father who was often away, too, looking for his fortune. It was a wonder to Pete that his father had finally settled at the Morgan ranch—but he was beginning to be glad that Pop had returned home. Perhaps not as glad as Pop was that his sons were slowly returning, one by one, to mend the past, but still, he was glad to be relearning how to love his father.

Suddenly the front door of the house flew open. A boy ran down the steps, jumping them two at a time. He was followed by two younger girls, who looked like they were trying very hard to keep up with their older brother, and an energetic black-and-white collie. Pete scooched down in his seat just a little, his eyes hungrily recording everything about the boy.

He was tall for his age, and obviously athletic. Pete held up a small camera, squeezed off a shot, checked it to make sure it was a good one. The boy was blond, like Priscilla, and his hair fell in straight locks of yellow-gold, flopping as he ran. His clothes were well made, neat, unlike anything the Morgan boys had worn growing up. Their mother had often sewn them clothes, or they'd worn each other's hand-me-downs. By the time a pair of jeans had gotten from Jack to Gabe, they were pretty worn. The boy threw a ball for the collie, who ran frantically to get it, and the girls ran after the dog, teasing it.

A woman came out onto the porch, shielding her eyes from the late afternoon sun. The February weather still held a chill, but the children didn't notice, despite the mother's urgings that they all should be wearing coats. After a moment she smiled, told them they could play another fifteen minutes only and went back inside.

The boy looked so much like Priscilla that it hurt Pete in a deep, unknown place. In another time, had Priscilla been able to make different choices, he might have been this child's stepfather. That would never happen now, of course. The child was happy here; he had a family who clearly loved him. Being the big-hero brother to two younger sisters was a great thing. Dane and Gabe had looked up to Pete on occasion, and he'd enjoyed the hero worship. One of the little girls fell, and her brother was there instantly to check her out. Pete heard him say, "It's just a scrape, silly," but his gesture belied his words as he rumpled his sister's hair and helped her to her feet. Then he grabbed the ball from the collie, throwing it one last time before leading his merry band into the house.

Pete had tears in his eyes when the front door closed behind them, leaving him alone in the cold on the family-friendly street.

He switched on his truck and drove away. Mission accomplished.

"I COULD SELL YOU the business," Priscilla said to Cricket, "but you're busy enough with your deacon duties. However, I thank you for asking." She put some dishes into a box, checked its weight to make certain it could be easily moved. She didn't want to fill any of the boxes too full with her precious china. "No financial favors among friends. If I'd been able to keep the shop, I wanted you to be my partner, but more of a silent partner. You do so much for the people of Fort Wylie it would be wrong to weigh you down with my tea shop, dear friend."

"Oh, Priscilla," Cricket said, "I am so sorry. You must be so upset."

"I was at first." She had been, but now a curious peace filled her. "There is more to life than serving tea and cookies and giving etiquette lessons."

Cricket pulled down some teacups from a shelf, laying them on a table so Priscilla could pack them. "Like helping raise four young children?"

Priscilla had thought long and hard about the babies. She thought about Josiah; she'd pondered her future—if there was one—with Pete. "I'm sort of going on faith, I suppose. But I feel my place is somewhere else for now."

"You're not leaving because of your parents' issues, are you?"

"No." Priscilla shook her head. "I visited them yesterday. My parents seem so relieved that everything is over. They feel as if the floor is swept clean, all their secrets are out, and they can move on with their lives. I think it was cathartic for the news to be out in the open." Priscilla smiled at Cricket. "To their great surprise, they found they had a lot of support. The friends who have loved them over the years remain their friends, which was their greatest worry. They had their house paid off, and with that secure, Dad says everything else will turn around in time."

Priscilla felt pretty lucky to have them as an example. From her parents, she learned that there was no such thing as true failure. They were prepared to learn from their mistake. "Though they're upset for me, that I'll have to give up my shop, I've realized that taking the extra loan to enlarge my business would have only stretched me too thin. I'd like to make another run at this one day, but in a different venue."

She'd miss her tea shop. But she'd still have her house, and that comforted her.

But what use was a house if it wasn't shared with people she loved? *Josiah would salute that sentiment.*

Pete had changed her view of what she thought was most important in life. She wanted to help him—at least as much as she could.

PETE HAD CONVERTED one of the bigger upstairs bedrooms into a large nursery. For now, the four babies would sleep where he could easily hear them. His room was across the hall. Later on, he would think about bedrooms for each of them, but for now, painting the room a soft yellow and putting up baseball and flower murals on the walls satisfied his need to keep busy as he waited for his miracle. He'd bought white cribs. He'd stacked tiny diapers on a bureau nearby. Formula, towels, pacifiers—everything the woman at the baby store said he'd need with tiny babies—he'd purchased in bulk.

And then on a dreary February day, Pete's life

changed forever as four young bundles of joy were delivered to the ranch. It was the most insanely wonderful thing that had ever happened to him—and it was also pandemonium.

Mrs. Corkindale oversaw the whole process, watching intently as the swaddled babies were brought inside much to Josiah's delight and Priscilla's wistful gaze. The whole family was there, right down to the children, who were eager to greet the new members of the family.

"I hope you know what you got yourself into, Josiah," Mrs. Corkindale said.

He grinned, his face lighting up. "Angels. That's what's come to my house."

She patted his shoulder. "I think you could use a personal angel, myself."

He shook his head. "I'm fine."

"Well, you know where I am if you ever need more resources. We're stretched pretty tight in the county right now, but we have no intention of abandoning these children. And you know, fost-adopting doesn't have to be a lifetime commitment."

"Bite your tongue!" Josiah exclaimed, and she laughed, going off to examine the converted nursery, leaving Josiah, along with Gabe and Dane, to watch as Pete lovingly placed each baby in the large playpen in the middle of the den. All four babies lay on their backs, snug in different-colored blankets. They were quiet now, but as they grew, the ranch would be a hubbub of activity. Pop had wanted the playpen close to his recliner so he could see the babies at all times. "Feels like Christmas," he said. "If Jack was here, it'd be perfect."

Pete glanced up at his father's words. He flashed a quick look at Gabe and Dane, who merely shrugged. There was nothing they could do about Jack. Pete had tried to bring his brother home. It would never happen.

But Pete had brought the babies home. He watched Priscilla, who, though stiff at first, seemed to be slowly warming up, examining each infant with a smile on her face.

As for Pete himself, his heart was fuller than he ever dreamed it could be. For every night in his life he'd spent in some cold, godforsaken hole in the world, or some hot, deserted lair, this gift from God made up for everything in life he'd missed out on.

And the fact that Priscilla was there to share the moment with him and his new family made it even more of a blessing. The situation was very nearly perfect.

It *would* be perfect—once he convinced Priscilla to marry him.

Chapter Fourteen

Babies didn't sleep much, Pete was quickly learning. The first night was a rodeo of sound, action, tears and quick reflexes. Every single member of the Morgan clan, as well as Priscilla, stayed at the house to be on deck for the real-life tutorial in how to take care of four babies. Josiah stated that it was like a bomb had gone off in the house, scattering the contents far and wide. It was every man and woman for themselves because the babies set the schedule.

This was the most fun Pete had ever had. He relished holding, feeding, comforting the babies. Even though he knew it was probably his imagination, he could already sense the personalities of each child. Two boys, two girls, all identical—and yet to him, each seemed unique. "I'm going to love being a father," he told Priscilla, who had stayed at his side all night assisting without complaint. "I already love it."

"I can tell." Priscilla gently picked up a girl he was

pretty certain he would name Angela. She was, after all, an angel, ceasing her tiny cries as soon as Priscilla held her. He didn't dare say that Priscilla would love being a mother—it would only add to her feelings of guilt over not being a mother to her son.

But he loved watching her with the babies, anyway. She was so careful, so precise. He'd made a good choice of a woman, or his father had. He glanced at Pop, who was eyeing him from under bushy brows.

"Good job," he told Pete, and Pete played innocent. "What job?"

"I know what you were thinking," Josiah said with a grin. "You were thinking you've got it pretty sweet around here."

"Let's not get carried away yet," Pete said, glad that Priscilla had taken Angela over to Laura for inspection. "She's tougher to corral than you think."

"Ah, well. Maybe the babies will help."

Pop didn't know the whole story, and Pete just left it that way. "Always good to have an additional plan of attack," he murmured.

To which Josiah said thoughtfully, "Yes, I believe you're right."

THE SECOND WAVE of reinforcements came two days later, and Priscilla was happy to see them. Laura and Gabe were going home with their children, and Suzy and Dane were, as well, since everyone had stayed the first two nights to help with the babies.

It had been a smoother transition than Priscilla had dreamed it might be. The community was pitching in, too, and it was great to see the "church ladies," as Josiah called them, pull up with groceries and homemade food.

"We couldn't wait any longer to see the angels," one woman said as she hugged Josiah's neck.

"Thank you," Josiah said gamely. "Glad to hear I've been promoted from sinner."

The woman smacked him playfully on the arm. "Show us the children, Josiah, and no more of your fishing for attention."

He proudly led the way. "This is the playroom," he said, showing them into the den. "Where I can play with them all I like."

"So it's *your* playroom," another woman observed, and he laughed.

Priscilla looked at Pete. "I think I smell apple pie."

"I think you do, and I'm pretty sure I caught a whiff of fried chicken." He watched as ten women filed in, all under Josiah's pleased gaze. "There was a time when people called my father simply 'Jackass' and not 'Josiah.'"

"Times change," Priscilla said.

"Do they ever."

The babies were in various stages of crying or being cooed over, and all were getting their share of gentle attention. The church ladies were more than happy to take over for a while.

"I'm going to shower," Priscilla said.

Pete glanced at her. "I could use a shower myself."

Was that a veiled invitation? She wondered. It surprised her, because Pete had to be as exhausted as she was. Plus, she needed time to process the events of the past three days. It had been a whirlwind of excitement and amazing moments with the babies, but she felt herself beginning to pull back, retract from the sense of family, the feeling of being a true part of the Morgan clan.

It was becoming harder than she'd imagined.

Sometimes she had to remind herself sternly that she was a fake fiancée and not the real thing—Pete was not going to be her husband. "I think I'll head upstairs," she said, breaking eye contact, dismissing any notion Pete might have had about joining her for a nice, soothing shower and a delightfully sexy rubdown afterward.

She just couldn't let herself think about that. It was all becoming too close to being home—with Pete.

JOSIAH'S PLAN C arrived on Saturday, and at the same time Mrs. Corkindale came by for a visit. Pete termed it a visit, because she came bearing a cherry pie and some wonderfully aromatic pot roast, just the right thing for the cold February day. Unfortunately the arrival of both parties at once made matters worse.

Pete would never know why his father called back the women he'd invited to his matchmaking party, but suddenly, he found the playroom swarmed by eager women, and Priscilla backing away like a turtle into a shell.

"Pop, what are you doing?" Pete demanded as the six women and Mrs. Corkindale all ended up in the den at the same time. Priscilla edged herself to the side of the group, relinquishing her place by the babies.

"Bringing in reinforcements," Josiah said.

"Do we need them?" Pete asked, and Josiah nodded.

"Trust me, son, I know what I'm doing."

Pete wasn't so sure. "I think it's too much noise, maybe even too many germs for the children," he said, thinking that these were all well-meaning people who would have to be trained to care for tender newborns. Plus Priscilla was eyeing the women like they were some toxic stew. They were clearly crowding her out.

And apparently Priscilla wasn't going to stand her ground. She slipped from the room after the introductions were made to place Mrs. Corkindale's offerings in the kitchen. Pete wondered about his father's intentions. He hadn't introduced Priscilla as Pete's fiancée, and bringing other women into the picture probably wasn't the Plan C Pete would have picked. "Another round of church ladies might have been more helpful, Pop."

But Pop grinned. "Not for what you need, son."

He winked at Pete, leaving Pete to ponder what it was his father thought he needed. He decided to ask.

"Why, you need help with these babies!" Josiah grinned. "Every one of these women has a résumé just right for nannying."

"Nannying?" Pete frowned. "Now, wait, Pop, there'll be no nannies for my children."

"Actually, you might find a nanny helpful," Mrs. Corkindale said. "I'm sure you'll have to go back to work eventually. Your father can't handle these four babies by himself, should the fost-adopt become permanent."

Pete hesitated. First, the fost-adopt would work out. He wasn't about to consider that it wouldn't. He squinted at his father, suddenly calculating the less-than-coincidental chance that Mrs. Corkindale and the matchmaking-party women had shown up on the same day. Pop was shrewd; he wasn't about to give Mrs. Corkindale anything to complain about. If anything, Pop would want the social worker to see that the Morgans had everything well in hand. Pete wanted to say that Priscilla would take care of the children, as would Pete when he wasn't working—but then, he couldn't exactly claim a traditional family.

He couldn't say Priscilla would stay home with the children, because she wasn't his wife, wasn't the children's mother, and they'd never discussed anything beyond the fake engagement. So that was out. And he *did* have to work eventually. The hiatus was simply a vacation of sorts. He knew he would be working within a year, although the job he wanted was right here in this room. Still, a man couldn't be Mr. Mom and Dad forever.

Pop couldn't handle the children by himself. In fact, he looked more gaunt than usual, although strangely cheered by Mrs. Corkindale's presence. Pete found that mildly astonishing. She didn't seem the sort to put up with Josiah's bullheadedness; however, he could imagine Pop making an effort to be pleasant to her for the sake of the babies.

More on that later, Pete decided. He couldn't worry about his father's love life with the amount of energy Pop devoted to Pete's. His father had a point—it would look better to the caseworker if he demonstrated his foolproof plan for caring for the babies. Priscilla had come back into the den, looking at him from outside the circle of women. The truth was, he was kidding himself if he included her in his life plan. He didn't know if she'd ever fall in love with him.

Maybe he was simply being too suspicious of Pop's meddling in his love life. "I guess you're right, Pop," Pete finally said. "Nannies are a great idea."

Yet it seemed the second he said the words Priscilla seemed startled, as if that was the very last thing she expected him to say.

PRISCILLA HAD PUT a lot of effort into pushing her guilt aside and trying to enjoy her time with the babies. It was easier than she thought it would be.

The children were darling heart stealers, so cute that even their tears were adorable. And she loved watching Pete with them. This was a man who was born to be a father, even if he'd never known it. The Morgans were all so busy trying not to turn into Josiah that they never realized they had awesome father potential. Even Gabe and Dane seemed thrilled with the new family members.

And Josiah was on cloud nine. So she was surprised—and a bit hurt—when all the women from Josiah's matchmaking party showed up. Privately she had considered this to be her and Pete's "honeymoon" with the babies, the time they needed to see if they could work out who they were and what they were to each other, and the children.

But the women…well, they couldn't have been more obvious about their designs on Pete. They weren't mean to Priscilla, but neither were they terribly warm, as they were to Josiah and Pete.

Yet Mrs. Corkindale seemed reassured by the backup plan Pete and Josiah apparently had for additional help, so Priscilla wasn't about to voice her doubts. If anything, she saw this as a new challenge. Would she be able to handle watching other women set their agenda for Pete? He certainly hadn't mentioned that she was his fiancée, nor had Josiah. And if Mrs. Corkindale wondered about that, she didn't say so.

The worst part was feeling like a visitor when she'd just begun to get used to feeling like part of the family.

No, that wasn't the worst part. The worst was feeling like Pete no longer needed her, now that he had his children safe under his roof. She'd begun to believe that she was Pete's choice, and now it was clear she was not.

Chapter Fifteen

"Are you a family friend, Priscilla?" Chara, a beauty with an old-movie-star type of glamour, asked, "Or are you part of the family?"

Priscilla hesitated, unsure of how to answer. Mrs. Corkindale stood close by, a smile on her face. The babies were all being stroked or attended to by one of the other women. Pete didn't say anything—just stood there with a big goofy smile on his face, and Josiah grinned like a fox in a henhouse. She couldn't ruin the ruse, so she finally met Chara's gaze—while the other women looked on with interest—and said, "I'm Pete's fiancée."

Immediate disappointment jumped onto all six women's faces. They glanced at Pete in surprise. He crossed his arms and said, "I'm afraid that's right. I'm taken, ladies."

Priscilla's jaw dropped. The ass! The jerk! He

sounded as if he was some kind of prize she'd won. She wanted to dump a pitcher of lemonade on his handsome head.

Instead, she said sweetly, "But there's always Josiah."

Josiah choked on his lemonade, glancing at Mrs. Corkindale hastily. "Not me. I'm wed to these babies for now. But I do have one more son."

The ladies perked up at that last bit of information, although Priscilla noticed they still cast longing eyes at Pete.

"Where's your ring?" Chara asked. "I'd love to see it, Priscilla."

"Ring?" Priscilla asked.

Pete quickly said, "We haven't picked it out yet. We've been a little busy." He gestured to the babies. "We'll get around to it, though, won't we, honey?" He put his arm around Priscilla's shoulders.

"I don't know," Priscilla said through gritted teeth. "We're so busy with the babies, *dear.*"

"Oh," Chara said, "well, congratulations. There's nothing like a small-town wedding, is there?"

"I'm sure there's not," Priscilla said.

"And aren't you fortunate to start off your marriage with four bundles of joy," Chara continued.

"Blessed, totally blessed," Priscilla said, stiffening. She was going to kill Pete for getting her into this. He could certainly put a stop to the cross-examination she was getting!

"I'll be available during the honeymoon," Chara said.

Priscilla stared at her. "For what?" she asked.

"To help watch the children, of course. I'd do anything to help Josiah. When he called and asked if I'd like to apply for the position of nanny, I jumped at the chance."

I bet you did, Priscilla thought. "How kind of you. I'm sure Pete appreciates your willingness. Anybody else for lemonade?" Pete reached for her as she moved away, but she skirted his touch. If he thought she was going to be sweet to him now, with all this drama he and his father had visited upon her, he could just plan on her being a lot more like lemons than lemonade, so to speak, from now on.

And he'd made that matchmaking party sound so boring! Clearly Pete was possessed of a silver tongue of which she'd been previously unaware. From now on, she'd know better when he tried to convince her that she was the only one who could help him attain his crucial desire.

"POP, YOU PROMISED. No more interfering." Pete knew something valuable had been lost this afternoon with Priscilla. He couldn't quite put his finger on it, wasn't entirely familiar with the female mind, but he'd sensed a greater reserve on Priscilla's part than ever before, just when he thought he'd been getting her to thaw.

Josiah looked at him. "Mrs. Corkindale seemed pleased that we had extra help. I think it's a good move, though I should have consulted you first. It's just that you've been so run off your feet with your new brood."

Possibly Pop was as innocent as he claimed, but Pete doubted it. "I don't think Priscilla was entirely comfortable with the horde of females around the place."

Josiah raised a brow. "Did she say so?"

"No. She's Miss Manners. Priscilla's never going to complain."

His father looked at him. "Son, it's time Priscilla gets to stating what she wants."

"And you thought you'd help her do that? Exactly what do you want her to say?"

"That she wants to be with you and these children. That she'd love to stand at the altar and become your wife. That's all I'm saying."

"It's none of your business, Pop," Pete said sternly. "Personally, I'm willing to march on Priscilla's time."

Josiah shrugged. "It's not like time is stored in a bottle around here, son. The sands of the hour glass and all that."

Pete looked at his father sharply. "Are you feeling under the weather? Not that I'm excusing what you did, but do you feel all right?"

"Will you be less annoyed if I said I was on my deathbed?"

"No," Pete said, "I just wouldn't believe you."

"Okay," Josiah said. "I hear a baby calling you. Maybe two or three." He grinned, glad to shift Pete's attention away from himself.

Pete pointed a finger at his father—the gesture was playful, yet meaningful. "Pop, I insist. Not one more instance of inviting single females to this house without my permission."

"Does that include Sara?" Pop asked, his gaze cagey.

"Sara?"

"Corkindale," Josiah told him, and Pete felt stupid.

"I never knew her name. She was always the social worker, Mrs. Corkindale, who held the key to my future."

"Yeah, well," Josiah said. "I've got to work all angles, you know."

"Oh. Is that what the older generation calls dating these days?"

Josiah tossed a magazine at him, but Pete had already escaped, feeling like he'd handily won this round with his father.

Now to win Priscilla.

THE FOUR BABIES had other designs on Pete's time. He never got a chance to speak to Priscilla about the women from the matchmaking party and why they'd shown up. He knew she needed some reassurance, at least an apology, but the babies were fierce in their desire to be coddled and nurtured while being assimilated into their new environment, so he had to put romancing Priscilla the way she deserved on hold until he got the care of the newborns under control. The babies didn't need a lot—just love, attention, food, diaper changing—but they demanded it around the clock.

Josiah wanted to be helpful, but he wasn't up to the pace. It was just Pete and Priscilla tonight performing a seemingly never-ending dance of diapers and comforting and feeding.

At last, however, Priscilla threw in the towel on the whole situation. It happened when she uncovered one of the platters that had been left in the kitchen. Many of their visitors brought food, but this particular visitor—from the matchmaking-party bunch—had also left him a note. The note basically invited him to call her if his fiancée should get cold feet.

And cold feet is exactly what Priscilla came down with. Which totally stank, because he had a fever, and Miss Manners wasn't in the mood to play nurse.

"It seems obvious you've worked out your backup plan," Priscilla said, "and I think it would be best for both of us if I left you to it."

"Ugh, don't do that," Pete said. "Chara sure isn't the one in the bunch I'd go for even if I wanted to."

Priscilla picked up her suitcase. "I've called a taxi."

He wanted to offer to drive her to Fort Wylie if she

was so bent on going, but there was no way he could leave the four babies with just his father. "You have no idea how much I want you to stay."

"It's hard, Pete," she told him. "I took a leap of faith here. I wanted to be a good surrogate mother. I wanted to be a good surrogate fiancée. It just doesn't feel right to me."

Thanks, Pop. If Pop had thought to force Priscilla into a more marriage-ready position with his antics, he'd not understood his prey this time. Miss Manners would never fight about anything. It just wasn't in her blood. "Priscilla, I don't have the skill I need to convince you that your place is here with me—"

"Oh, I think you're quite smooth with words." Priscilla shook her head. "I'm not angry, Pete. I just don't feel my place is here."

"Let me change your mind." He took her in his arms, kissed her forehead. "I don't think you liked Dad's friends."

"Because they want to be *your* friends." She sighed. "And I don't want to make this about petty jealousy, either. I'm certain that under different circumstances, those women and I might get along fine. It just felt incredibly awkward."

"You need an engagement ring," he said.

"No, that won't exactly solve it."

"What would, then?"

She moved from his arms. "If I were a different woman."

He didn't like the sound of that. "But you are who you are and I like you."

She shook her head. "It's hard to explain."

Suddenly he knew what she was thinking. "You believe that you were doing your best to overcome your guilt as a mother, and then Pop sprung a bunch of women on you, and now it would just be easier to move away from trying to get over what happened when you were younger."

"I don't know if I'm that good at analyzing myself."

He kissed her on the lips, gently. "I do analysis."

"Do you?"

"Yeah. It was part of my job. Always good to know your target."

"Great. Now I'm wearing a bull's-eye," Priscilla said.

"I've got one right over my heart." He placed her hand against his chest.

"Don't romance me, Pete," she said softly, in the rare moment of calm when babies weren't needing them. "I know you'll be fine without me, and I really do have some things to work out."

"I'm asking you to take a big step," Pete said, "so I've tried not to rush you."

"And yet I feel like I can't quite catch up to you."

He sighed. "I wasn't going to show you this yet. I was going to wait until…God, I don't know when I was going to show you. But I think maybe this will help. I hope it will."

Gazing into her eyes, wondering if he was making the right decision, Pete slid the photograph of her son and his sisters from his wallet, handed it to Priscilla.

She studied it for a moment, then glanced up at him. "Who are they?"

"That's your son," Pete said, "and those are his little sisters."

Her eyes grew wide, her gaze jerked back to the photograph. "My *son?*" Priscilla murmured, her whole body stiffening, and then without warning, before he even had a chance to perceive her reaction, Priscilla grabbed her bag and hurried out the front door.

He stared after her, stunned. Outside a car door slammed, and he heard the taxi pull quickly away.

So much for knowing his target. The photograph lay on the floor where Priscilla had dropped it as if it was white-hot—but the only thing on fire right now was his heart.

Chapter Sixteen

Priscilla's life changed forever the moment she saw her son in the photograph. She sat in the taxi feeling almost winded. Unexpected tears poured down her face. Anger filled her—anger at Pete for ripping off the scab, anger at herself for giving her son away, anger at her parents for insisting it was for the best.

"Where to, ma'am?" the cabbie asked.

"Fort Wylie," she replied, and gave him her parents' address. She needed family around her now—*her* family—and maybe even some answers. She needed time. Her brain could barely register what she'd seen.

She was furious with Pete for snooping around in her past. How dare he play God, like his father?

Pain seeped into her heart. Her son. She told herself perhaps Pete had located the wrong child, yet she knew enough about Pete to know he would never make that error. Her son was a beautiful child. Any mother would be proud. She was proud, and yet she felt so utterly lost.

Unfortunately she also felt an overwhelming desire to hold him just once, tell him that not one single day in her life had gone by without her thinking of him, wondering if she'd made the right decision. Clearly she had, if his smiling face was any indication. She was still struggling to figure herself out financially—he would not have grown up in the type of house seen in the picture. Nor would he have had the two sisters he seemed quite close to.

She closed her eyes, prayed the pain would recede.

How dare Pete intrude in her life this way? And what exactly had he hoped to gain? She knew him well enough to know that he was a Morgan, and Morgans, she'd learned, didn't do anything without hoping to gain from it.

It had something to do with the babies. Perhaps Pete labored under the misguided belief that if she knew her son was happy, she could move on with her life.

The notion might be good on paper, but it didn't take into account the layers of guilt in her subconscious over giving up a child, and she doubted Pete could ever understand how deeply a mother's heart suffered.

Josiah was just as bad—Pete had obviously learned from his father. She had no idea who'd thought it was a good idea to bring in all the extra female assistance, but she'd guess it was Josiah. With Mrs. Corkindale approving so much of the additional help, Priscilla could hardly protest. Yet she couldn't help feeling pushed out, unneeded. Perhaps *less needed* was the correct term. Definitely replaceable, like a piece of china. Josiah wanted six pieces of china, instead of just one, in case that one broke. Maybe it was a fail-safe plan, and maybe Josiah and Pete needed that kind of security in their lives.

She leaned her head back, willing herself not to think of anything more than the cold, starlit evening and the fact that she'd be home soon enough, with time to think about exactly what had happened today.

All she knew was that she wanted desperately to see her son now—and she knew she never could. She would never forgive Pete for cruelly opening up this deep wound in her heart.

"IT'S GOOD TO SEE you, Priscilla," Rosalie Perkins said, hugging her daughter. "We know you've been very busy."

Priscilla walked into her parents' home. "I should have come sooner."

Her father, Phil, shook his head. "We were too busy wrapping up paperwork to have had time to visit. We're just glad you're here now."

They went into the kitchen and sat where they always sat—at the small table in the kitchen nook. Rosalie put out glasses of iced tea for them, and Priscilla thought about the many times over the years this ritual had been performed. It was comforting, and yet, she didn't feel comforted.

"How was Union Junction?" her father asked.

"Busy," Priscilla said carefully. "The four newborns at the Morgan ranch keep everyone very busy."

Her mother smiled. "I hope it works out for them."

Priscilla decided she wouldn't mention her own part in the plan that helped in the success. Why get her parents all excited about an engagement that would never be? "So everything came out all right with the bankruptcy?"

"It did." Phil nodded. "Everyone's been very understanding."

"The worst part was having the notice in the paper," Rosalie said. "It's so embarrassing to have your financial situation laid bare for everyone. But we're getting ourselves back on the right track now."

"With help from Charlie Drumwell, things have been going well," Phil explained. "That's one smart young man."

Priscilla didn't want to comment on that, but her mother said, "You never did mention how your date went."

"It was fine," Priscilla said.

"Such a nice man," her mother said on a sigh. "You could do worse, Priscilla."

"Mom, Dad," Priscilla said suddenly, "I've tried to do a lot with my life since the mistake I made when I was a teenager. I haven't dated a lot, I haven't—"

"Priscilla," Rosalie said, her tone distressed. "Have some more tea."

"All I'm saying is that everyone makes mistakes.

But mine was a baby, not necessarily a mistake. Why were you so insistent that I give my son away?"

The room went silent. On the wall, the kitten clock ticked. Priscilla could hear her own heartbeat in her ears.

Her father cleared his throat. "You were very young, Priscilla. You had a lot of life ahead of you. We didn't want you saddled with the responsibility."

She thought about the picture of her healthy, happy son. "I feel like I've lost something critically important in my life."

"I know," Rosalie said. "We both think about it all the time, honey."

Priscilla looked at her mother. "Do you?"

"Of course," Rosalie said carefully. "That was our only grandchild, you know."

Phil nodded. "But ten years ago, that was a decision we didn't think you should have to make. It would have meant giving up your childhood, Pris."

"So I gave up his." Priscilla grabbed a tissue off the counter. "I know he's happy, but—"

"How do you know that?" Rosalie asked.

"I—I just do." Priscilla shook her head. "I just think some of our decisions have the ability to affect the rest of our lives. That one affects me."

"Oh, dear," Rosalie said unhappily, "of course it does. Our financial decisions will always affect us, the mistakes we made, the things we wish we'd done better. Life is full of decisions that never quite leave us. But we did the best we could in advising you about that matter, Priscilla. It's not something we can undo now."

Priscilla thought about her son, happily playing with his two little sisters in front of the big house. "I know," she said softly. "But that doesn't make it any less painful."

"Maybe spending so much time with those Morgan babies has upset you," Phil said. "Kind of brings the past back a bit, don't you think?"

"Not directly," Priscilla murmured, and yet it had. Her father was right. She'd always agonized over her decision, but it was kept in a closet deep inside her. Now that secret was out, bringing its painful questions with it. "I felt guilty just holding the babies."

"Oh, my," Rosalie said, and burst into tears.

Priscilla shook her head. "I'm sorry, Mom."

"Well," her father said, "I don't know what to tell you, Priscilla, except that you're a good girl. We know everything will work out for you eventually. And we're sorry that the bankruptcy hurt your tea shop. Hurting you was the last thing we intended."

Rosalie wiped her eyes with a tissue. "We thought we were making the best financial decisions, ones that would help you after we're gone."

"Don't say that!" Priscilla exclaimed. Instantly she thought of Josiah, who didn't look all that strong to her, though he might have been tired from all the activity in the house. "Everything is going to be fine.

Let's not talk about this ever again. There's no reason to. And don't ask me about Charlie, either," she said on a sigh. "We really didn't suit."

"Because you already had a crush on that cowboy," her mother said. "We heard all about him from Cricket."

"Oh," Priscilla said. "Let's not talk about him, either."

"All decisions are not bad ones," her father said. "Sometimes they require a little more time for the good in them to be revealed."

Priscilla shook her head, not about to be drawn into a discussion of Pete. Nor did she want her parents weighed down with their daughter's private pain; they had enough of their own right now. She opted for safety, knowing it was good to return to the things they found traditional and comforting. "I'll get the cookies out. And it's such a cold night, does anyone feel like working a puzzle in front of the fireplace?"

"WHERE'S PRISCILLA?" Josiah demanded the next day. He watched the church ladies take over so that Josiah and Pete could take showers and rest for a bit. The babies had treated them to an active night, and Pete could honestly say he was looking forward to a good long nap.

"She went home," Pete said.

"Any reason she deserted us?"

Pete hesitated. He wanted to talk about what had

happened, but he wasn't sure about hearing Pop's reaction. One thing about Josiah is that he wouldn't pull any punches. "She didn't exactly desert us."

"She couldn't have been that bothered by a little competition," Josiah said. "I had her marked for more grit than that."

"Not sure about that, but I can say it didn't help. However, I'm afraid I'm the culprit here." His father and he took seats outside on the patio, despite the chill. Josiah said he needed fresh air, and fortunately they were on the south side of the house, where the sun shone. A chimenea smoked nearby, throwing a little warmth and the scent of burning wood, which Josiah liked to huddle near. To keep his father from getting too cold, since he did like to sit out on this patio and look over his land more and more these days, Pete had installed a propane heater near their chairs, which also emanated heat. "I looked up Priscilla's son."

Josiah's head reared back. "What are you talking about?"

"She had a son when she was seventeen. She had to give him up for adoption, and she never got over it. It was one of the reasons she wasn't altogether sure of herself when it came to the babies, whom I've named, by the way."

"Oh?" Josiah asked, momentarily sidetracked.

"Yes," Pete said, happy to have his father off the painful subject of Priscilla for the moment. "Josiah John—"

"Ah, good one," Josiah said, suddenly looking misty. "Good of you to name one after Jack."

"You and Jack, Pop," Pete said. "We can call him Joe. Or Jack. Doesn't matter."

Josiah smiled. "Can't say I haven't waited a long time for that, son."

Pete nodded. He knew. He understood. They'd all been on such difficult terms for so long, no one would have thought to name a child after ornery Josiah. But so much had changed for Pete. "And then there's Mary Angela, Michael Peter and Michelle Gisella."

His father looked at him. "Named after your mother."

Pete shrugged. "Seemed right. If we get to keep them, those will be their christened names."

"Good," Josiah said, pleased. "Although you know that Dane and Gabe will feel left out since you picked Jack's name and not theirs."

"They have their own namesakes, or have them on the way," Pete explained. "I don't think Jack ever will."

Josiah sighed. "Don't depress me, son. Now, back to your conundrum. I have a feeling it's a doozy. You never were one to do things halfway."

"This is true." Pete reflected on his father's words ruefully. "I thought that if Priscilla knew that the son she'd given up was happy and healthy, maybe she could forgive her teenage decision and grow to love these children like her own."

"Uh-oh," Josiah said. "You should have asked my

advice before you meddled, son. You're not very good at it yet."

"True as that may be, I located the boy. He's a good kid. Bright, healthy, happy. Has a great home, great family. Nothing to regret there." It still bothered Pete just a wee bit that he could have been the child's stepfather had life turned out a little differently. "I didn't talk to him, of course. I took a photo and I left."

"Let me get this straight," Josiah said. "Priscilla's been dealing with her parents' financial difficulties, her own financial issues and giving up her tea shop, and then coming out here to help you by pretending to be your fiancée, and then you go and spring her past on her."

Pete looked at his father. "I believe that just about sums it up."

"Son, you ran that girl off."

"Don't tell me that," Pete said. "I've come to really like her a lot."

"I know," Josiah said. "So, Pete, what were you thinking?"

"I was thinking I could take away some of her pain," Pete replied honestly.

"Were you? Or were you living your own past, remembering how it was when your mother left you," Josiah said. "Were you thinking that you'd love for your mother to ride up one day and erase all the lost time in your childhood? And maybe that little boy would, too?"

Pete blinked. His father's words arrested him. He walked through them again slowly, replaying them in his head. "You're suggesting that I put myself in her son's shoes?"

"With a mother who abandoned you," Josiah said bluntly. "You never got over that, and I suspect you were assuaging your own pain rather than Priscilla's."

"I hope not," Pete said. "I never meant to hurt her."

"Yeah, but sometimes the past needs to stay in the past, son." Josiah leaned closer to the clay chimenea, tucked his blanket around his legs. "I suspect you're still a little angry with me, too, which you haven't resolved."

There might be some truth to that. Pete shrugged. "I think we're getting along better than ever in spite of my doubts."

"But you've never forgiven me for your mother leaving. You think that if I'd treated her better, paid more attention to her, she would have stayed. And that might be true," Josiah admitted. "In your mind, I'm still the jackass no one wanted to be around. But you can't fix this for Priscilla. If she doesn't want to be the mother to your children, you'll have to accept that. You can't dig around in her past and paste it together and make it good."

Pete stared at the chimenea. He didn't know what to say, didn't know what to think anymore.

"So she up and left," Josiah said.

"I showed her the photo, and she took off like a shot. She was ready to leave, had already made up her mind about that, due to the women here and how they made her feel. But then I suppose I capped off the moment by trying too hard to fix it. Keep her here." Pete hung his head, rolled his neck, tried to release some tension. It wasn't going to leave him anytime soon.

Josiah sighed. "Pete, my tough guy, superspy, secret-agent son, I hope you can take what I'm about to say."

Pete stared at his father. "Bring it on."

Josiah shook his head, patted his son on the shoulder. "My guess is you don't see that girl again."

The words cut deep, but Pete didn't answer. There was a faint ringing in the hollow of his heart that warned that his father was probably right.

"If it makes you feel any better, and it probably won't at this moment," Josiah said, "I've decided to transfer your million dollars into your account tomorrow. You'll need it for the little ones, and while you haven't been here a year, I'm real proud of what you've accomplished. You've brought the spirit of family into this house."

Pete reached over and patted his father once on the back. "Thanks, Pop. I appreciate your belief in me." It felt good after all the years of separation to have Pop's faith. Pete leaned back in his chair, staring moodily at the fire, thinking about Priscilla, his temporary fiancée who was more temporary than fiancée.

Chapter Seventeen

It had been a week since she'd left Union Junction and Priscilla still felt somewhat lost. Everything in her life seemed to have shifted.

She walked into her closed tea shop and flipped on a light. The tables and chairs needed dusting. Her answering machine was full of messages, but she didn't want to listen to them right now. Knowing that people were still interested in teas and the services she provided should have made her feel better.

A knock on the door made her look up. Cricket's anxious face peered through the glass. Priscilla smiled and went to let her friend in. "You're a welcome sight."

Cricket blew in on a swirl of brisk wind. "Wow! It's nippy out there! Hey, I knocked at the house first, then figured you were in here."

"Let's see if the teakettle still works, shall we?" Priscilla said. "Maybe there're some frozen cookies I can defrost."

"Don't trouble yourself for me," Cricket said, hugging her friend. "I just wanted to check on you."

Priscilla locked the door behind Cricket. "I'm glad you did. Lay your coat over a chair and let's chase the ghosts out of the kitchen."

They found cookies and heated water for tea, then seated themselves at a table in the dining room where the lights wouldn't be obvious to any passersby. Priscilla didn't want anyone to think the shop was reopening.

"How have you been?" Cricket asked, and Priscilla shook her head.

"Life is mysterious," she said. "Let me tell you about the babies first."

"Please do!" Cricket grinned. "Are they perfection?"

"More than perfection," Priscilla told her. "Seashells for toes, buttons for noses. You can't imagine anything more darling. Even when they cry, even when they burp, they are so…so amazing."

Cricket stared at her. "You're in love with them!" she exclaimed, delighted.

"I know." Priscilla laughed. "You can't hold them and not fall deeply."

"What about their father?" Cricket asked. "Do you fall as deeply when you hold him?"

Priscilla didn't know how much she was ready to tell. "Can I talk to you as my deacon?"

Cricket looked at her. "Of course. Deacon and friend."

Priscilla took a long time to consider her words. She cupped her suddenly cold hands around her teacup, tried to steel herself to share her secret. "I had a baby when I was seventeen."

Cricket didn't appear shocked. She just listened. So Priscilla moved on. "I gave him up for adoption."

Her friend leaned over to hug her. "I am so sorry for everything you've been through," she said.

Tears seeped from Priscilla's eyes and ran down her cheeks. She couldn't speak. She didn't want to wail like a baby, but that was how she felt, as if a good, shuddering cry would release all the pain she'd been repressing. "I held myself back from Pete because of that. I felt so guilty about my own child that I couldn't think about being a mother to another. I agreed to be his pretend fiancée so he would look better to the adoption people—they'd prefer a traditional family. But all the time I knew I would never marry him, could never be the mother to those orphans."

Cricket patted her hand and leaned back in her chair. "Priscilla, you are such a strong woman."

"No, I'm not," she said. "I'm in love with a man I can't marry because I have no intention of being a mother to his children."

"So you left," Cricket said, and Priscilla nodded.

"I had to. At first I told myself I was leaving because of the women who were there. Remember the matchmaking-party attendees?"

Cricket nodded. "Well, we never met them, but I remember not being invited to the party until Suzy called us."

"Yes, sneaky of her." Priscilla wiped away her tears and gathered her composure. "I told myself I was jealous of them, that they made me feel less a part of the family. But I've had a week to think about it, and I believe I was only using them as an excuse to separate myself from Pete."

"We do those things," Cricket said.

"So I'd already ordered the taxi," Priscilla continued, "and then Pete pulled out this photograph of my son. My whole world fell right through the floor."

Cricket's eyes widened. "I bet. I don't even want to think of where my world would have dropped."

Priscilla's eyes darkened as she remembered. "He's the most beautiful boy," she said, her voice distant. "I can tell he's an amazing child. Sensitive, caring, kind. And I'll never get to know those things about him."

"Oh, dear," Cricket said. "Priscilla, don't torture yourself, honey."

"I try not to. But I've held it in the back of my mind for so long that confronting it is tearing me apart."

"What did Pete say?"

"I can't remember. I just left. I know he meant to help, but…"

"And yet, aren't you glad you know?"

Priscilla hesitated, then nodded. "I am glad to

know that my son is all right. That he has a good family. That he's happy."

Cricket sipped her tea, tested a frozen cookie to see if it had thawed enough. "Sometimes in life we're given a second chance."

Priscilla was too afraid to let hope slip into her heart, though Cricket's words were like oxygen to her.

"What I mean is, you did nothing wrong. In fact, you did the right thing by allowing your son to find a home where he would be loved." Cricket let those words sink in for a moment. "For as long as we've been friends, I've known you to be an honest, kind, hardworking woman. I've been proud to call you a friend. I believe God gives us second chances, and those babies are yours to love."

Priscilla looked at Cricket, barely daring to hope. "Do you think so?"

Cricket nodded. "Of course. Why would you not be a wonderful mother?"

Priscilla hoped she would be, wanted to be.

"Did you feel that you didn't deserve another child?"

"I… Yes," Priscilla murmured. "I was certain I would never marry a man who wanted children as badly as Pete Morgan did."

"Well," Cricket said, "he's already got the children, honey. I'd say all you have to do now is take the ready-made family and believe that you were meant for them as much as they were meant for you."

Priscilla sat frozen, thinking, praying, hoping.

"You said you love Pete, right?" Cricket asked.

Priscilla nodded slowly. "I think I did from the moment he first teased us. Remember when he burst into the house at the ranch in January? I thought he was the most dashing, devil-may-care man I'd ever seen."

Cricket smiled. "I remember. He packs a powerful punch. Lucky for you I've got an unrequited thing for his brother, or the matchmaking bunch aren't all you'd have to worry about."

Priscilla smiled. "Loving Pete happened so quickly."

"Then don't let him get away," Cricket told her. "It's not every day a woman finds a man with a heart of gold and four little angels to love."

"I don't know what to do," Priscilla said, but Cricket smiled.

"I do," she said. "You're going to have to meet him on his terms."

WHEN PRISCILLA returned to the ranch, she found Mrs. Corkindale and the matchmaking bunch in residence. It took courage, but she walked in the front door like she was part of the family.

Pete greeted her with a hug. "Awfully glad to see you."

She smiled at him gratefully, then went to kiss Josiah's cheek.

"Good to see you, gal," he said gruffly, and Mrs. Corkindale smiled.

The four babies lay in a large playpen, silent for once. Their eyes blinked and their fingers flexed into small fists occasionally, but for the moment, they were peaceful. "They look like they're settling in well," Priscilla observed.

"I have the sense that leaving the hospital helped," Pete said. "Here there's relative calm."

She nodded, glad when he took her hand and pulled her outside. "Can you watch the babies for a minute?" he called over his shoulder to the women.

"I see you're not lonely," Priscilla said, "and I'm glad of that."

"Have you forgiven me?" Pete asked, and Priscilla looked at him.

"I think so," she told him honestly. "I know you were just trying to help me."

"I swear I was," Pete said. "But I also recognize it wasn't my place to do that. I've got my own family tree to locate if I want to hunt someone up."

She took a deep breath. "On that subject, I want you to take me to see him."

Pete blinked. "See him?"

"My son."

"Is that a good idea?"

"I don't know," she said. "But just once I'd like to see him with my own eyes. I don't want to talk to him, I don't want to upset his world. But just once, I've got to see him." She swallowed. "I need to know."

Pete held Priscilla in his arms. "I've opened up a

Pandora's box for you. If I could take that back, I would."

She shook her head. "Believe it or not, you may have done me a huge favor."

"I was only doing it for me," Pete said. "I wanted you to be free of the past so I could have you all to myself."

"I don't know if that's possible," she admitted, "but I know I won't give you up without a fight."

"Oh, don't worry about them," Pete said, jerking his head back toward the house where the matchmaking bunch was. "They're not interested in me as much as they are Pop's money, I think. Nice girls, but I'm not quite the catch Pop paints me."

"You're probably not," Priscilla said, teasing. "But I meant I would fight with *myself* to not give you up."

"Ah," Pete said, "I hope you win. There's a great prize for the woman who wins me. It's called the Four Babies plus Bachelor Bonanza."

Priscilla raised a brow. "Don't forget the crusty father-in-law, who by the way, seems to have a frequent female caller."

"I think he and Mrs. Corkindale get on well," Pete said. "When do you want to leave to see your son?"

Now, she wanted to say. *Five minutes ago. Ten years ago.* But she just looked at Pete, and he nodded.

"Okay. We'll leave in the morning. You realize, doing this will probably change you forever. How can it not? This is coming from a guy who understands something about shifting family dynamics."

Priscilla felt like her breath was being held by an invisible hand. Being changed forever was part of life. She wasn't afraid of that. What she was afraid of was never seeing her son—and that was what had always haunted her.

Chapter Eighteen

Priscilla stood outside the pretty house where Pete had driven her, shaded by an oak tree that hung over the street. Pete believed that the school bus would arrive around this time, and if Priscilla's son didn't take the bus, surely his carpool or his mother would arrive with him. This was Priscilla's best chance at getting a glimpse of her son.

She felt a bit like a stalker, but since she had no intention of speaking to him or making herself obvious, she cut herself some slack. She knew she would never come back here. It wouldn't be fair to herself or to her son. It was now or never. Pete understood this and had parked the truck a short distance away; he was nearby but still gave her space.

Suddenly a school bus pulled up, just as Pete had hoped, and a little boy got off, then turned to help his two younger sisters off. He waved to his friends as the bus pulled away. Priscilla's heart jumped into her throat. Her son took a soccer ball from his backpack, kicking it from one foot to the other. His sisters tossed down their packs, ready to play, so he gently kicked the ball their way.

A woman came out on the porch, and they all ran to hug her. Priscilla expected jealousy to tear into her, but what she felt, instead, was deep, humbling gratitude as she watched the ritual. After each child was hugged, they went back to playing. The woman called, "It's cold out here! Don't you want to come in for cookies and cocoa?"

"In just a minute, Mom!" the boy called. "The girls need to practice their kicking."

The girls looked to be only six or seven years old, Priscilla estimated. She was proud that her son deemed himself his sisters' coach.

Suddenly one of the girls misfired her kick and the ball rolled into the street. Priscilla's heart lurched; she forced herself to stand still. This was likely not the first time this had happened; the boy would know what he was permitted to do when his ball rolled into traffic.

"Stay right there, you two! Okay? Stay right there. I'll be right back." Her son carefully checked both ways—setting a good example for his sisters—then headed across the street to retrieve the ball. It would have rolled right to Priscilla had she been standing in the street, instead of on the sidewalk.

"Hi," the boy said, surprising her. He'd come to stand beside her to wait for the street to clear again.

"Hello," Priscilla said, drinking in his face and the

smell of him. He had her blue eyes and the slope of her nose, and he smelled like a warm little boy who played a lot at recess and was probably good in gym class. "Nice kicking."

He smiled. "Thanks. I'm trying to teach my sisters."

"Good job."

He still waited for a break in the traffic. "I like soccer, but I'm going to be a doctor when I grow up. Or a math teacher."

"Both of those sound wonderful," she said, her heart twisting. "Good luck. You'll be awesome at either."

He looked her full in the face, and at that moment Priscilla saw that she had made the right decision all those years ago. Her son was happy, he was carefree, he was loved. And he would grow up to be whatever he dreamed of being.

"Bye," he said as the street cleared.

"Bye," she said, watching him run back across the street and toss the ball to his waiting sisters. "Goodbye, my son," she said softly, and then turned to walk toward Pete's open arms.

Chapter Nineteen

Pete had been apprehensive about taking Priscilla to see her son, but the woman who returned with him to the Morgan ranch was a different woman altogether. She couldn't seem to wait to hold the babies. She didn't care about the matchmaking bunch; in fact, she seemed to understand how much more comfortable Josiah felt to have a veritable throng of people in his house. Priscilla was relaxed and happy, and if she every once in a while turned reflective, he understood why.

The old hesitant Priscilla who kept herself in a tea shop and held etiquette lessons was gone. In her place was a woman who sparkled with life and generosity, and the babies were clearly recipients.

"What did you do to her?" Josiah demanded. "Is there something going on I should know about?"

"I don't think so," Pete said, watching Priscilla hover over Mrs. Corkindale as the older woman diapered one of the babies.

"That was some car ride you two took. Did you ask her to marry you?"

Pete shook his head. "Nope." But maybe it was time he did. Maybe she was ready to think about other changes in her life, some that included him in a permanent capacity.

"If I were you, I'd shop for a ring," Josiah told him. "I'd get it on her finger as fast as I could. Strike while the iron's hot and all that."

Pete shook his head. "There's no hurry, Pop."

"Sure there is. Women have moods."

Pete laughed. "So do men."

"Yeah, but women marry when they're in the mood. Men marry when it's practical."

"Don't worry, Pop. It'll all work out."

"I know what changed," Josiah said. "You told her about the million dollars."

Pete raised a brow. "Didn't you once say Priscilla was the only person you knew who didn't have a price?"

Josiah wrinkled his nose. "That was before I met Sara." He jerked his head toward the social worker.

"You didn't try to bribe her on my behalf, did you, Pop?" Pete demanded, and Josiah sighed.

"Son, some habits are hard to break."

"Did you ever think that might have hurt my chances of getting the babies?"

"Nah," Josiah said. "I bribed her with some sugar, which she seemed to like well enough."

Pete stared at his father, and then had to smile.

"You ought to try it," Josiah said.

"I just might," Pete replied, before going to drag Priscilla away from the babies.

"I SHOULD BE helping Mrs. Corkindale and the women," Priscilla said as Pete walked her outside, but he shook his head.

"You should be helping *me,*" he said. "Pop's driving me nuts."

"Oh?" Priscilla glanced at him. "What's he up to now? I've been keeping an eye on him and—"

Pete cut her off with a kiss. "You know Pop. The itinerary is never quite clear."

"That's what I like about him. He's full of surprises."

"He is that." Pete took her hand in his, leaned against a fence. "Pop seems to think you need a little sugar."

She looked up at Pete. "I remember you playing spin the bottle in January in the kitchen using a bottle of vanilla with Suzy, Cricket and me. I thought then that you probably needed some sweetening. So I suggest it's not me who needs the sugar, cowboy."

"Oh, really?" He wore an amused smirk on his face, and she knew he remembered spinning that bottle, too.

"Yes, I told you I wouldn't kiss a man I didn't plan on marrying, and you spun that bottle elsewhere real fast."

He laughed. "Seems like the bottle came back your way. And I still think a little sugar wouldn't hurt you at all, Miss Manners."

"Well, it will depend on whether you're offering one lump or two," she told him, arching a brow at him.

He grinned. "How about a two-carat lump?" he asked, pulling a jeweler's box from his pocket.

She gasped, and then waited with big eyes for him to open it. "Don't keep me in suspense, Pete!"

Chuckling, he opened the box. "Priscilla Perkins, it would give me the greatest pleasure on earth if you'd become my *real* bride, my best friend and the mother of all my children. I've loved you from the first time I saw you, all prim and proper and tempting. Back in January, when you and Suzy and Cricket were baking cookies and you snapped my butt with that dish towel, I knew you were the kind of woman who could keep me perpetually on my toes. I know that sounds crazy, but I like a woman with a little sass and a lot of heart. I don't think I'd ever get over it if I couldn't have you to share my life. So what I'm trying to say is—" he took a deep breath "—Priscilla, will you marry me?" He was down on one knee as he said the words, and he had a clear vision of the joy in her eyes.

"I might," she said, a little devilish merriment in her eyes. "Let me see if this ring fits."

He knew she couldn't wait to get the ring on her finger, and the knowledge thrilled him. Still, he was content to go along with the teasing a little longer—he wanted this to be one of the biggest moments of her life, one she would remember forever. "Aren't you supposed to say yes and then we get the ring sized?"

"I haven't read the etiquette book on that," Priscilla said, then watched as Pete slid the ring onto her finger. "Oh, Pete, it's *beautiful*. And it fits perfectly!"

Of course it did—he had memorized every inch of this woman, and he planned to refresh his memory for the rest of his life by loving her over and over again. "I was thinking you might like Cricket to perform the ceremony," he said.

She turned her rapturous gaze to him. "I would love that. Right here at the Morgan ranch," she said, "so your father won't have far to travel and we won't be far from the children."

"So is that a yes?" Pete asked, and Priscilla stood on her toes to kiss him on the lips.

"Of course. I love you," she told him. "I loved you the first time you slid into my life, bringing chaos and distraction and a lot of fun."

"I've changed," he told her.

"So have I, thank goodness," she said.

"I have a feeling we'll go through a few more changes," he said, and Priscilla smiled at her secret-agent lover. Being with Pete and the children made her dreams come true. The most wonderful part, the fairy-tale part, was that they'd be with each other forever as true husband and wife—and there was nothing secret about that.

Please join Pete and Priscilla Morgan
at the Morgan ranch
for a light reception to celebrate
their adoption of four angels
and witness the christenings of
Josiah John, Mary Angela, Michael Peter,
and Michelle Gisella
on March 15 at 3:00 a.m.
God has blessed our family in so many ways

*There's one Morgan brother left!
Jack is the most secretive of the brothers—he's
the eldest and most mysterious. A rodeo rider
who thinks he can't be tied down by anyone,
Jack learns how much family means to him
in THE TRIPLETS' RODEO MAN,
Tina Leonard's final book in
THE MORGAN MEN miniseries.
It's coming in March 2009, only from
Harlequin American Romance!
Turn the page for a sneak peak....*

Prologue

"You reap what you sow."—Josiah Morgan to his four sons, a general reminder

Late March, Union Junction, Texas

Jack Morgan stood at his father's bedside in the Union Junction hospital, staring down at the large sleeping man. Josiah Morgan had the power to impress even in his peaceful state. Jack couldn't believe the old lion was ill. He didn't think Pop had ever had so much as a cold in his life.

But if his brother Pete said Pop was weak and in need of a kidney transplant, then those were the facts. Jack took no joy in his father's situation, even though the two of them had never been close. He hadn't seen Pop in more than ten years, not since the night of his rodeo accident, his brothers' car accident and the all-out battle he and Pop had waged against each other.

It had been a terrible night, and the details of it were still etched in his mind. And then there was the letter he'd received through Pete from his father just last month.

Jack, I tried to be a good father. I tried to save you from yourself. In the end, I realized you are too different from me. But I've always been proud of my firstborn son.
Pop

As patriarchal letters went, it stank. Jack figured Pop wouldn't have sent a letter at all if he wasn't sick, so he'd decided to come see for himself. He hadn't expected to care what happened to the miserly old man; Josiah was miserly with his affection, miserly with his money, time, everything. At least that was the father Jack remembered. Still, Jack preferred his father fighting.

"All right, Pop, you old jackass," Jack said, "you can lie in that bed or you can fight."

One eye in the craggy face opened to stare at him as he spoke, then the other opened in disbelief. "Jack," Josiah murmured.

A thousand emotions tore through Jack. "Yeah. Get up out of that bed, old man."

"I can't. Not today. Maybe tomorrow," Josiah said gamely.

"Damn right," Jack said. "Because if I'm giving

you one of my kidneys, I expect you to be jumping around like a lively young pup."

Josiah squinted at him. "Kidney?"

"Hell, yeah," Jack said. "You and I might as well be tied together for a few more years of hell—don't you think? It could be the one thing we have in common. We're apparently the perfect match for a kidney swap, which I find amusing in a strange sort of way. Not any of my brothers—me, the perfect donor match for you. It's almost Shakespearean."

His father shook his head and closed his eyes. "I don't want any favors, thanks."

Jack pulled a chair close to the bed and sat. "No one's trying to do you a favor, you old jackass, least of all me. Quit feeling sorry for yourself, because I sure as hell don't."

Josiah's eyes snapped open, sparks shooting at his son. "No one has ever felt sorry for Josiah Morgan."

Jack nodded. "Glad we got that settled. You'll need to be in the right frame of mind to get healthy for all those brats you thought you needed."

"Brats?"

"You've been bringing children into the family faster than popcorn popping. Pretty selfish of you to drag all those kids in here and then send up the white flag of surrender, don't you think, Pop?"

"I didn't ask to have rank kidneys!" Josiah barked.

Jack stretched his legs out in front of him, legs that had seen a few sprains and breaks from bulls that had taken out their own rage on him. "We all make our choices."

"I did not choose this."

"You've been 'self-medicating' for years. It's one of the reasons I don't touch a drop of liquor. I decided long ago not to live by your example."

"Alcohol didn't give me kidney disease." Josiah pulled a whiskey bottle from under the sheet and took a swallow he would have deemed "just a drop."

"Sure didn't help it, either." Jack stared at his father. "Pitiful, if you ask me."

"Well, I didn't ask," Josiah snapped, secreting the bottle again.

"It's nice to be able to tell you exactly what I want while you lie there captive. I've waited years for this moment."

Josiah looked at his son. "I guess you think paybacks are hell."

"I guess so, Pop." Jack wasn't about to give his father an inch of sympathy. The old man was mean as a snake. All the charity and benevolence he'd been throwing around in the past few years didn't fool Jack. Josiah Morgan didn't do anything without a motive.

Josiah shook his head. "So many years passed, and you didn't even let me know you were all right. You chased the one thing you cared about all your life—rodeo—and at thirty-two, you decide you're going to give up the one thing that matters to you? You can't ride with one kidney. It'd be foolish."

"I'll take the risks I want, Pop." Jack stood, staring down at his father. He didn't like the old man, would never forgive him for the harsh words over the years. Wouldn't forgive him for never being proud of him. Wouldn't forgive him for blaming him for the car accident his brothers had been in the night Jack had been carted to the hospital. "It's a kidney, Pop, and I'm not doing it for you. I'm doing it for my brothers, who are bringing up the families you've saddled them with. You ought to live to reap what you've sown."

"I'm proud of what I've sown!" Josiah shouted after him as he departed. Jack kept walking. It was a kidney he was giving up, not rodeo. Pop had it all wrong.

* * * * *

Harlequin is 60 years old,
and Harlequin Blaze is celebrating!
After all, a lot can happen in 60 years,
or 60 minutes…or 60 seconds!
Find out what's going down in Blaze's
heart-stopping new miniseries,
FROM 0 TO 60!
Getting from "Hello" to "How was it?"
can happen fast….

Here's a sneak peek of the first book,
A LONG, HARD RIDE
by Alison Kent
Available March 2009

"IS THAT FOR ME?" Trey asked.

Cardin Worth cocked her head to the side and considered how much better the day already seemed. "Good morning to you, too."

When she didn't hold out the second cup of coffee for him to take, he came closer. She sipped from her heavy white mug, hiding her grin and her giddy rush of nerves behind it.

But when he stopped in front of her, she made the mistake of lowering her gaze from his face to the exposed strip of his chest. It was either give him his cup of coffee or bury her nose against him and breathe in. She remembered so clearly how he smelled. How he tasted.

She gave him his coffee.

After taking a quick gulp, he smiled and said, "Good morning, Cardin. I hope the floor wasn't too hard for you."

The hardness of the floor hadn't been the problem. She shook her head. "Are you kidding? I slept like a baby, swaddled in my sleeping bag."

"In my sleeping bag, you mean."

If he wanted to get technical, yeah. "Thanks for the loaner. It made sleeping on the floor almost bearable." As had the warmth of his spooned body, she thought, then quickly changed the subject. "I saw you have a loaf of bread and some eggs. Would you like me to cook breakfast?"

He lowered his coffee mug slowly, his gaze as warm as the sun on her shoulders, as the ceramic heating her hands. "I didn't bring you out here to wait on me."

"You didn't bring me out here at all. I volunteered to come."

"To help me get ready for the race. Not to serve me."

"It's just breakfast, Trey. And coffee." Even if last night it had been more. Even if the way he was looking at her made her want to climb back into that sleeping bag. "I work much better when my stomach's not growling. I thought it might be the same for you."

"It is, but I'll cook. You made the coffee."

"That's because I can't work at all without caffeine."

"If I'd known that, I would've put on a pot as soon I got up."

"What time *did* you get up?" Judging by the sun's position, she swore it couldn't be any later than seven now. And, yeah, they'd agreed to start working at six.

"Maybe four?" he guessed, giving her a lazy smile.

"But it was almost two…" She let the sentence

dangle, finishing the thought privately. She was quite sure he knew exactly what time they'd finally fallen asleep after he'd made love to her.

The question facing her now was where did this relationship—if you could even call it *that*—go from here?

* * * * *

Cardin and Trey are about to find out that
great sex is only the beginning....
Don't miss the fireworks!
Get ready for
A LONG, HARD RIDE
by Alison Kent
Available March 2009,
wherever Blaze books are sold.

CELEBRATE
60 YEARS
OF PURE READING PLEASURE
WITH **HARLEQUIN**®!

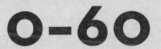

We'll be spotlighting a different series
every month throughout 2009
to celebrate our 60th anniversary.

Look for Harlequin® Blaze™ in March!

0-60

*After all, a lot can happen in 60 years,
or 60 minutes...or 60 seconds!*

Find out what's going down in Blaze's
heart-stopping new miniseries *0-60!*
Getting from "Hello" to "How was it?"
can happen fast....

*Look for the brand-new **0-60** miniseries in March 2009!*

www.eHarlequin.com   HBRIDE09

You're invited to join our Tell Harlequin Reader Panel!

By joining our new reader panel you will:

- Receive Harlequin® books—they are FREE and yours to keep with no obligation to purchase anything!
- Participate in fun online surveys
- Exchange opinions and ideas with women just like you
- Have a say in our new book ideas and help us publish the best in women's fiction

In addition, you will have a chance to win great prizes and receive special gifts! See Web site for details. Some conditions apply. Space is limited.

To join, visit us at

www.TellHarlequin.com.

REQUEST YOUR FREE BOOKS!
2 FREE NOVELS PLUS 2
FREE GIFTS!

American ★ Romance®

Love, Home & Happiness!

YES! Please send me 2 FREE Harlequin® American Romance® novels and my 2 FREE gifts (gifts are worth about $10). After receiving them, if I don't wish to receive any more books, I can return the shipping statement marked "cancel." If I don't cancel, I will receive 4 brand-new novels every month and be billed just $4.24 per book in the U.S. or $4.99 per book in Canada. That's a savings of close to 15% off the cover price! It's quite a bargain! Shipping and handling is just 25¢ per book, along with any applicable taxes.* I understand that accepting the 2 free books and gifts places me under no obligation to buy anything. I can always return a shipment and cancel at any time. Even if I never buy another book from Harlequin, the two free books and gifts are mine to keep forever.

154 HDN EEZK   354 HDN EEZV

Name _____ (PLEASE PRINT) _____

Address _____ Apt. # _____

City _____ State/Prov. _____ Zip/Postal Code _____

Signature (if under 18, a parent or guardian must sign)

Mail to the **Harlequin Reader Service:**
IN U.S.A.: P.O. Box 1867, Buffalo, NY 14240-1867
IN CANADA: P.O. Box 609, Fort Erie, Ontario L2A 5X3

Not valid to current subscribers of Harlequin® American Romance® books.

Want to try two free books from another line?
Call 1-800-873-8635 or visit www.morefreebooks.com.

* Terms and prices subject to change without notice. N.Y. residents add applicable sales tax. Canadian residents will be charged applicable provincial taxes and GST. Offer not valid in Quebec. This offer is limited to one order per household. All orders subject to approval. Credit or debit balances in a customer's account(s) may be offset by any other outstanding balance owed by or to the customer. Please allow 4 to 6 weeks for delivery. Offer available while quantities last.

Your Privacy: Harlequin is committed to protecting your privacy. Our Privacy Policy is available online at www.eHarlequin.com or upon request from the Reader Service. From time to time we make our lists of customers available to reputable third parties who may have a product or service of interest to you. If you would prefer we not share your name and address, please check here. ☐

HAR08R2

HARLEQUIN® *Romance*®

This February the Harlequin® Romance series
will feature six Diamond Brides stories featuring
diamond proposals and gorgeous grooms.

Share your dream wedding proposal and you could WIN!

The most romantic entry will win a diamond
necklace and will inspire a proposal in one of
our upcoming Diamond Grooms books in 2010.

In 100 words or less, tell us the most romantic
way that you dream of being proposed to.

For more information, and to enter
the Diamond Brides Proposal contest, please visit
www.DiamondBridesProposal.com

Or mail your entry to us at:

IN THE U.S.: 3010 Walden Ave., P.O. Box 9069, Buffalo, NY 14269-9069
IN CANADA: 225 Duncan Mill Road, Don Mills, ON M3B 3K9

No purchase necessary. Contest opens at 12:01 p.m. (ET) on January 15, 2009 and closes at 11:59 p.m.
(ET) on March 13, 2009. One (1) prize will be awarded consisting of a diamond necklace and an author's
fictional adaptation of the contest winner's dream proposal scenario published in an upcoming Harlequin®
Romance novel in February 2010. Approximate retail value of the prize is three thousand dollars ($3000.00
USD). Limit one (1) entry per person per household. Contest open to legal residents of the U.S. (excluding
Colorado) and Canada (excluding Quebec) who have reached the age of majority at time of entry. Void
where prohibited by law. Official Rules available online at www.DiamondBridesProposal.com. Sponsor:
Harlequin Enterprises Limited.

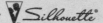
™ *Silhouette*®

SPECIAL EDITION

Kate's Boys

TRAVIS'S APPEAL
by *USA TODAY* bestselling author
MARIE FERRARELLA

Shana O'Reilly couldn't deny it—family lawyer
Travis Marlowe had some kind of appeal. But
as Travis handled her father's tricky estate
planning, he discovered things weren't what
they seemed in the O'Reilly clan. Would
an explosive secret leave Travis and Shana's
budding relationship in tatters?

Available March 2009
wherever books are sold.

www.eHarlequin.com

SSE65440

BRENDA JACKSON

TALL, DARK… WESTMORELAND!

Olivia Jeffries got a taste of the wild and reckless when she met a handsome stranger at a masquerade ball. In the morning she discovered her new lover was Reginald Westmoreland, her father's most-hated rival. Now Reggie will stop at nothing to get Olivia back in his bed.

**Available March 2009
wherever books are sold.**

Always Powerful, Passionate and Provocative.

www.eHarlequin.com

SD76928

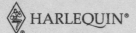

HARLEQUIN®

American ★ Romance®

COMING NEXT MONTH
Available March 10, 2009

#1249 THE SHERIFF OF HORSESHOE, TEXAS by Linda Warren

Men Made in America

Quiet, friendly Horseshoe is the perfect place for Wyatt Carson to raise his young daughter. Until Peyton Ross zooms through his Texas hometown, disrupting his peaceful Sunday and turning his world upside down. The irrepressible blonde is tempting the widowed lawman to let loose and start living again. But there's more to this fun-loving party girl than meets the eye....

#1250 THE TRIPLETS' RODEO MAN by Tina Leonard

The Morgan Men

Cricket Jasper knows Jack Morgan's all wrong for her. But that doesn't stop the virtuous deacon from falling for the sexy rodeo rider. The firstborn Morgan son came home to make things right with his estranged father. Now *he's* about to become a father. Whoever dreamed it would take a loving woman with three babies on the way to catch this roving cowboy?

#1251 TWINS FOR THE TEACHER by Michele Dunaway

Times Two

Ever since Hank Friesen enrolled his son and daughter in Nolter Elementary, Jolie Tomlinson has been finding it hard to resist the ten-year-old twins...*and* their sexy dad. The fourth-grade teacher is happy to help out the workaholic widower—but getting involved with the father of her students is definitely against the rules. Besides, Jolie doesn't know if she's ready to be a mother—not until she tells Hank about her past....

#1252 OOH, BABY! by Ann Roth

Running a business and being a temporary mother to her sister's seven-month-old are *two* full-time jobs. The last thing Lily Gleason needs is to be audited! Then she meets her new accountant. Carter Boyle is handsome, single and trustworthy...and already smitten with Lily's infant niece. But the CPA has a precious secret—one that could make or break Lily's trust in him.

www.eHarlequin.com

HARCNMBPA0209